PIECES OF US

AASHU KANDOI

Made with ♥ on the Notion Press Platform
www.notionpress.com

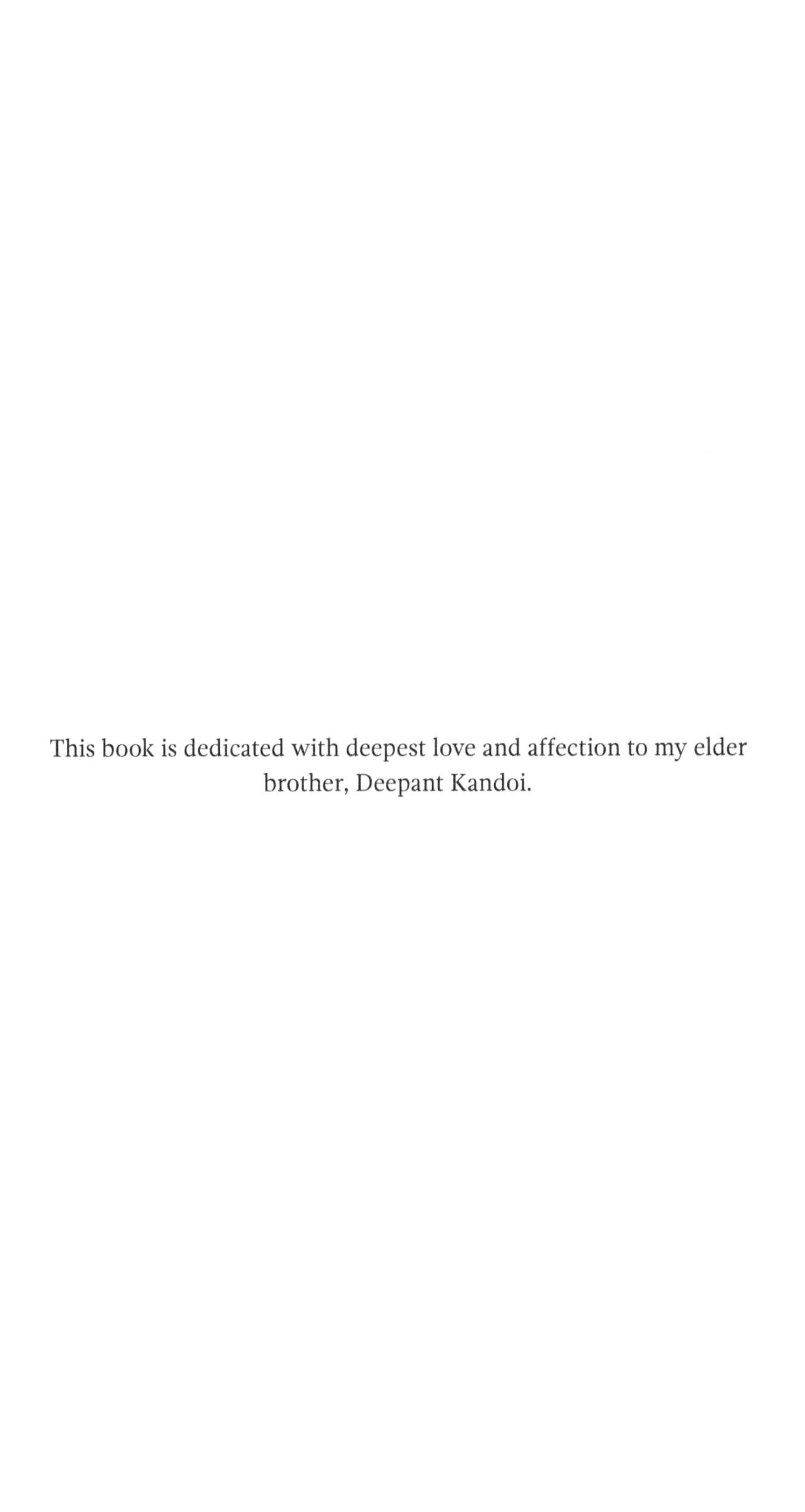

This book is dedicated with deepest love and affection to my elder brother, Deepant Kandoi.

Contents

Contents

Acknowledgements

THANK YOU - Dear Reader & Friend,

For picking up, PIECES OF US

A huge THANK YOU to all those people who have shaped me into this human being I am right now & accidentally shaped this book as well.

<u>Family</u>: Parameshwar Kandoi, Ramchandra Kandoi, Renu Kandoi, Sanjay Kandoi, Sumit Kandoi, Rashmi Kandoi, BrajGopal Kandoi, Deepant Kandoi, Richa Kandoi, Drisha Kandoi, Krishna Kandoi, Sonam Kandoi, Subh Kandoi, Nabh Kandoi, Anjali Kandoi, Renisha Kandoi, Aman Kandoi, Harshika Kandoi, Rishabh Kandoi, Subham Garg, Sneha Garg, Ayush Kejriwal, Divya Saraff, Rupa Gadia, Manoj Gadia, Kanhaiya Agrawal, Renu Agrawal, Roshan Agrawal, Sikha Agrawal, Raju Goel, Sanjay Goel, Shrishti Agrawal, Pankhuri Agrawal, Khusi Pashari, Pihu Bajaj

<u>Friends</u>: Aashutosh Singh, Arunav Karna, Manish Saini, Raghav Bakshi, Sohan Jha, Beevash Jaiswal, Ravi Shah, Aashiq Shah, Munna

Paswan, Riya Sinha, Ayushi Singh, Payal Chanani, Sonu Mittal, Niharika Kharel, Shipli Singh, Sanchita Bhattacharya

Please, forgive me if I forgot to mention your name. Trust me, you are equally important.

Introduction

To be brutally honest, this book was not meant to be written at this time. However, an unplanned retirement from my 18 years long cricket career left me with plenty of time on my hands.

Apart from learning the nuances of my family business, I decided to employ this additional clot of time in writing my third book. Initially, I had minimal idea about the structure and theme of this book. However, as Martin Luther King Jr. had said *'You don't have to see the whole staircase, just take the first step'*, I did the same. I followed his footsteps. And boom!

This piece of heart was born.

I hope you will enjoy it.

I hope you will cherish it.

I hope you will treat it as every heart deserves to be treated, *with love & affection.*

CHAPTER I

Ludo-Partner

कोई पूछे अगर, मेरी सबसे हसीं खता,

उस सुबह, तेरा हाथ थामना याद आता है

"Aapko bhaiji stage pe bula rahe hain," she reminded me gently.

'Haan, bas,' I replied before rushing off.

The photo session had begun after the *Varmala*, a much anticipated event in any Indian wedding.

I'm not sure why, but these photo sessions always remind me of a zoo. People keep staring at the newly married couple in a manner they would stare at the wild animals and birds; scrutinizing their tiniest of moves. Random photographs are clicked without their consent. The couple appear to be caged like the creatures behind the bars. They have no alternative but to smile and pose.

I didn't have an option either. Arjun, the groom, my friend, would have killed me if I didn't participate.

I hopped onto the stage reluctantly. Dheeraj & Balram had already flanked Arjun from the right side. Obviously, we didn't want to stand between the couple. Abhinav & I slid swiftly to the left of Shweta bhabhi.

Posing for a photograph has never been my forte. Holding on to an expression is really difficult for me. Over the years, I've created a standard expression to use whenever the need might arise. My standard expression includes an uncanny habit of putting my arm around the person I am posing with and a baby smile showing my not so white teeth.

This time though, I restrained myself from putting my arm on her shoulder. I was not sure how she would take it. I was not sure how others would take it. I decided to focus on getting my baby smile right.

Understandably, Arjun didn't have much time to attend to me. Still, he found me among the crowd after the photo session.

"Had your dinner," he investigated, looking a bit jaded.

'Not yet,' I answered.

"Then have it. You must be hungry after your fierce *baraat* dance."

His smile told me that he was pleasantly surprised with my uncharacteristic display of the dancing skill.

'Yes. My engine certainly needs some re-fueling,' I quipped, circling my stomach with my hand.

I am sure I saw him chuckle.

"There is a separate arrangement for vegetarian dinner. Take an exit from the main gate, turn left, walk 30 paces. You will reach your destination," he instructed me.

A robust man with a towel wrapped around his head, sitting alone & idle was pleased to see someone visit his counter. He graciously dished out some 'daal', 'bhaat', 'aalu-tarkaari', 'rasgulla' in a paper plate.

We were in a small village named Nirmalli in Bihar. It was not an extravagant wedding by any means. Each penny was calculated and spent meticulously. Generally, in Rajput communities, the groom is entitled to demand a fat sum of money if the groom has some prestigious degree or holds an important position in the society. A Doctor can command upto 50 lakhs plus car, washing machine etc; Government Officer 50 lakhs; Bank PO 20 lakhs; Clerk 10 lakhs; Any Other Government Job Holder 10 lakhs.

No, it's not dowry. It's an old tradition.

My dear friend Arjun Singh was eligible for the 10 lakh category. He was a teacher in a government school. But he had chosen not to make any monetary commandments. 'It's not right. Marrying someone for money is like doing a transaction,' he had said to me.

I was eating at my own steady pace when a fragile figure approached towards me. It was too dark to recognize the figure.

"Hurry up bhaia, it's already 11 o'clock. We need to go," Dheeraj appealed.

I gobbled up the remaining food in no time. We took our luggage and informed Arjun about our departure.

"How can you go now? *Phera* is yet to be done. Marriage is not complete yet!" he argued.

"We have some important pending work tomorrow morning. We need to return anyhow,' Balram countered.

Arjun looked at me with dwindling hope in his eyes.

"Okay. Let them go. I am not letting you go anywhere. I don't want to be alone. I need you," he uttered in a cracked voice.

'If they head back now, how will I go tomorrow?' I retaliated.

"I will manage that," he shot back.

Even I wanted to be with him on his Big Day. The problem was, Dheeraj will take the car with him & no one else was staying back. Besides the issue of the vehicle to return home, there was also a high chance of me getting bored without any friends. I was in a conundrum. A four month old conversation with Arjun sprang up into my head just in time.

'I might not be able to make it. I need to attend a family wedding on March 27.'

'Oh!! In that case, I will shift my wedding date to May 24. Will that be okay?'

'Yes. That will be great.'

How could I dishearten a man who had postponed his wedding date only for my presence? How could I let down a man who has made me feel so special? Emotions are my top most priority. These little gestures are priceless for me.

'Alright. Don't worry. I am not going anywhere. I will stay back,' I said without wasting any time.

That relieved look on his face filled me with delight.

Soon, we were on the terrace of the bride's house, metres away from the wedding place. Four slanted bamboos converging at one point on the top were tied together to make up a temporary mandap for the Phera. A senile punditji, adjusting his dhoti, took the centre stage. He instructed the couple to sit in a particular arrangement and started offering the sacred prayers.

Chairs & mattresses were sprayed around for the audience. I surveyed the whole area to find some acquaintances. I found none.

I went to the farthest corner. It was less crowded. Occupied a vacant chair. Waking up till 12 AM was not something I was accustomed to. I was sleepy, very sleepy. My mini doze attacks were not letting me watch the proceedings.

"You are still here!!" Abhinav broke my slumber.

'Yup. I didn't want to leave Arjun alone. I thought you had departed too. So glad to see you. Have a seat,' I put my hand on the adjacent unoccupied chair.

Suddenly, I saw her, the same girl who had asked me to meet Arjun on the stage, appear out of the staircase. She moved forward with zest. There was a bounce in her short quick steps. My eyes were wide open now. She looked elegant in an onion colored sleeveless gown which had a big black flower printed just below her right shoulder. A black colored dupatta hanging vertically from her left shoulder which had golden leaves embroidered on it at a distance from each other highlighted her fair complexion superbly. And the golden colored jhumkaa completed her traditional look perfectly. A gang of girls of her age was already occupying the mattress quite close to me. She joined them.

I re-coiled my attention on punditji reciting the sacred mantras. It got too boring after a point. My eyeballs strayed away automatically for a split second.

She was staring at me. I didn't know how to respond. I turned my head in a flash but the corner of my eyes remained on her. I tried to act as if I didn't notice her. She was still looking at me. I had never faced such a situation before. I scooped my phone from my pocket, unlocked it, swiped twice & locked it again.

I knew most of the members from Arjun's family except this girl.

Thank god, she was looking elsewhere now. This time, I gathered some courage to look at her directly. She ran a hand through her hair, tucking a strand of hair behind her ear. And then, she typed something in her phone and smiled at it.

Three girls from the gang vanished, abruptly, leaving the space empty.

Pushpak joined her.

Pushpak is Arjun's aunt's son. He is a talker. He just needs an opportunity. He got one in me. We got engaged in a conversation quickly.

"You are a cricketer, right?" she chipped in without any warning.

'Yes,' I replied.

'Do you know how to play the helicopter shot?' she caught me off-guard this time.

I smiled.

'Not yet but I am planning to learn it very soon.'

She giggled, sounding remarkably girlish.

In order to kill time, I proposed to Pushpak an idea of playing ludo in my HTC desire 620G. He agreed. Abhinav poured in his consent. We dethroned our chairs & sat alongside Pushpak. We were about to start the game.

"I will also play," she announced out of nowhere.

In the middle of the wedding, four of us got intensely engaged in a game of ludo.

She was hunting me from the outset. Everytime she got an opportunity, she sent my token back into its yard even if it was not the cleverest of moves.

"I will not let you win at any cost," she threatened me. The statement took me by surprise.

'Let us see,' I challenged her.

The dice seemed to be favoring me in this clash. I got a chance to send her token back to the yard. Before I could tap on the token I needed to move, she tapped on the other token hurriedly.

'This is cheating,' I protested.

Although, disappointed, I found this act cute.

She wrinkled her nose and grinned.

Abhinav emerged as the winner. Three of us were fighting for the remaining slots now. All her tokens were resting back inside the yard. Her chances of securing the second position were meagre. She stood up sharply, 'I am not playing anymore!!'

'You can't leave like this!!' I opposed.

'I can,' she chortled.

Meanwhile, Abhinav pointed towards the bride & groom who were getting ready for the *pheras*.

We had to leave the game unfinished.

My friend had stepped into a new phase of his life; the role of a husband.

Pushpak told me that the tentative time to depart in the morning was 9 o' clock. We didn't have much time left. We figured out we could squeeze a 3-4 hour nap in the remaining time.

The room allotted to us was full of people sleeping in strange positions. We took a tour of all the other rooms. Fortunately, Arjun's room was unlocked. It was too messy but unpossessed. We drifted into a deep slumber.

'Wake up buddies, time to go,' Arjun woke us up.

We wanted to comply but these eyes!! They refused to give in so easily.

Pushpak entered into the room. He was the official caretaker - responsible to wake everyone up, get them freshen up and ready for the breakfast on time.

We obliged.

She darted in wearing a red check shirt, a black jeans and elegant black heels with an open toe looking as fresh as a daisy despite the lack of sleep.

Her dressing sense is nice, I thought.

Arjun looked a bit tense.

'What happened bhaiji?' Pushpak showed his concern.

He didn't respond.

'Don't worry. We are almost done. Pushpak bhaiji will take care of the rest of the things. Don't stress yourself,' she consoled him.

As close friends do, instead of consoling, I passed a comment on Arjun, 'You are so unappeasable. Hopeless fellow!!'

She turned towards me. Our eyes locked in for a brief second.

'You are absolutely right,' she said while folding the scattered clothes on the bed.

'Anyway, leave all this. Bhaiji, give me 500rs. for the recharge,' she extended her hand nonchalantly.

Arjun left the room shaking his head in disbelief.

'Can we play ludo if it's not getting late?' I laid down a proposal.

Pushpak descended down the bed, on the mattress I was lying on, alongside Abhinav. She enrolled herself again, as the last participant.

Amidst the game, she started discussing politics of Bihar with Pushpak.

'You people discuss politics too!!'

It was refreshing to see a girl discussing politics.

"We discuss anything and everything," she replied. I must admit I was more focused on her facial features than her reply.

She was stalking me once again.

'C'mon. Why are you chasing me?'

"My wish," she answered with authority.

Her condition was quite terrible again. She stood up to leave the game one more time.

This time, I grabbed her wrist, instinctively. 'I am not letting you go again. Sit down and finish the game first,' I pulled her down.

To my surprise, she sat down, submissively.

To my surprise, I could never think of doing this to a girl that too in front of her brothers.

The winner was about to be discovered when a shrill voice called out for Pushpak. He had to shoot off.

"I will be back in a minute," she ran after him, leaving us stranded again. Unanimously, two of us decided to bequeath the game & follow them.

Soon, we found ourselves in Arjun's in-laws house.

"Breakfast is almost ready. Please, have a seat," Pushpak requested.

We took our seats.

"Can this ludo be played online?" she asked me, forwarding her phone.

'Of course'. I peeped into her phone & taught her the procedure.

'Open the ludo king app. Click on 'play with friends'. Click on 'create room' to generate a room code. Share the room code with any person you want to play with. As soon as the person joins the table using your code, the game begins. '

Two young boys sneaked in with plates in their hand and placed it on the table for us.

We were more than happy to eat 'dahi chura', the easy-on-the-stomach meal after yesterday's heavy dinner.

In the meantime, she started discussing her studies with Pushpak.

'What do you study?' I intervened.

"Bachelor in Economics, final year."

'Where?'

"Darbhanga."

'Oh! What are your future plans?'

"Let's see. I will try for Delhi College Of Engineering or IIT."

'Great. My brother is an IIT pass out and also an alumni of DCE. Do tell me if you need any help.'

"Why not!! I need some preparation material for the entrance test of DCE and some guidance for IIT."

'I will try. I will ask my brother and let you know. Save my phone number and don't hesitate to ask for any other help.'

"Sure", she punched my number in her phone and joked, "should I save your name as ludo-partner?"

'Your wish,' a wry smile escaped my lips. 'By the way my name is Aarush.'

"I know that," she said, in an alluring voice.

"What's up mates! Breakfast done?" Arjun stormed in, a tad agitated.

'Yup.'

"Come aside then, I have something important to discuss with you."

He took me to the adjoining room, devoid of any human presence.

"Yaar, I have chosen the wrong girl I think!" he grumbled in a dejected tone.

'What happened?'

"We had an argument. She speaks so rudely."

'Oh! That's the reason you looked worried a little while ago!!'

"Yes."

'Look. Don't panic. It's an arrange marriage. Both of you barely know each other. Give it some time. Don't start judging her so early. Let her be. It will be alright. I am sure.'

"Really?"

'Without any doubt.'

"Hope so."

'What's the update on my return plan?' I prompted, attempting a change of topic.

"Don't sweat it. I've got it covered. You can come along with us in the car."

'When will you guys depart?'

"I never knew there are so many rituals in our culture!!" he swung his head from side to side.

I sensed an opportunity to tease him, 'I guess, you will discover a lot of things for the first time.'

"Hahaha. I guess it will take one more hour," he tried to deflect it this time.

'In that case, I will return back with Abhinav on his bike.'

"Are you sure? A 5 hour journey on a bike won't be tiring?"

'Yaa. Yaa. No issues. We don't have too much luggage. We will be fine.'

"Okay. You should be leaving then. No point delaying."

After a deep hug, we trudged out of the home. Abhinav was all set up with his bike roaring on the lean unprocessed street. We were surrounded by homes from both sides. She was sitting on the stairs of one of those closeby homes.

"You stay in Nepal, right?" she tossed an unexpected question at me.

I felt unprepared. The only word I could say was 'Yes'.

"The momos at your place must be delicious. I love to eat momos," she continued.

'Not really. It's not that good where I stay. You will find much tastier momos in Kathmandu, an overnight journey from my place.'

"Oh!! In that case can you bring it for me, the next time we meet?" she bantered.

I found this request crazy. Nevertheless, It's good to talk crazy at times.

'Sure. I will bring it next time,' I annexed the banter.

We broke into laughter before bading goodbye.

I didn't have the slightest idea that the journey home would be so gruesome. While making the decision to return on bike, I'd forgotten to account for our lack of sleep. The initial 80 kms on the National Highway no. 27 was not too laborious. As the journey progressed, it became more and more scary. I'd started snoozing. Even the headphones failed to keep me awake. Only the sharp little head jerks hitting my chest brought back my consciousness temporarily.

'Stop the bike, Abhinav,' I urged him.

"What happened?" he enquired.

'I am feeling too drowsy. I might fall from the bike any moment. Either you put me in an auto or stop the bike right here,' I demanded.

"Don't leave me alone brother. My eyes are heavy too. I think we should talk and keep ourselves awake," he came up with a solution.

We did try it. We also splashed some cold water on our eyes when we stopped at a confectionery shop to fill our stomachs. But these cures proved to be very short-termed. We still had to cover a distance of 60 kms.

It seemed too risky to continue our journey in this half-awake state. An accident was not too far away.

Luckily, somewhere, we found a chowki lurking outside a house. Without any second thoughts, Abhinav stopped the bike. A power nap of 30 minutes helped us regain our composure. We felt fresh and confident about reaching home without doing any damage to ourselves in the remaining 24 kms.

Finally!!

We made it. Thank God!!

No prizes for guessing what would have been the first thing that I had done after reaching home.

I slept. Like a log.

I felt so invigorated when I woke up. The heaviness in the head was completely gone. I felt as light as a feather. It was dark outside. I picked up my phone to check the time. I had been sleeping for nearly 4 hours. The clock showed 8 p.m.

A Whatsapp notification popped up.

SHE: Don't forget to help me out

ME: I do remember. Don't worry

I replied with a smile plastered on my face

SHE: ThankYou

ME: Thumbs up

SHE: Btw, nyc to meet you:)

ME: Same here:)

SHE: Ha. Main hu hi itni pyari. Bs kbi ghmnd nhi kiya:)

She replied cheekily

ME: Dis sounded like u were dying to say it:)

I tried to pull her leg

SHE: Nhi

ME: Haha..I giv u d benefit of doubt
SHE: :)
ME: Got to go now. Bye. Good Night
SHE: Bye. Good Night. See you soon.

CHAPTER II

Daddy

तेरा साया न होता अगर, हम कब के जाते बिखर

दरख़्त-सा खड़ा रहा तू सर पर, हर मौसम हर पहर

I entered the class.

I felt intimidated.

My previous class consisted of only 3 desks aligned in 1 column. 3 boys used to sit on the front desk, 3 boys in the middle and a solitary girl on the last desk.

Here I was, standing in front of 5 rows and 10 columns of desks.

I looked around. Students were scattered all over the class. No one was quiet. No one was still.

I felt absolutely isolated, surrounded by a mob of strangers.

Quietly, I moved forward with my school bag, which was less of a bag and more of a 'jhola with a zip', dangling in my hand. The jhola's exterior had small black and white squares printed on it, similar to a chess board. I was pretty uncomfortable with my jhola.

After a brisk contemplation, I decided to place the jhola on the desk of the 3rd row & 5th column. I did not want anyone to notice it. I did not want to sit in front and become the centre of attraction. I did not want to sit at the back either because my grandma used to say 'back benches are occupied by bad students' and I was not a bad student by any stretch of imagination. Although I did fail in mathematics in the entrance test of this school, I was an extremely bright student in my backyard, always securing the 1st position in every exam.

'Wait! Wait! You have failed in school!?' asked Ved in a tone full of curiosity.

Ved is my younger son. He is totally determined to quit his studies. We are chilling at home, in the lobby, having a casual conversation.

"Yeah."

'How did the failure feel, dad?'

"To be honest, I felt like digging a hole & hiding in it. It was embarrassing. It was my very first experience of failing. I remember having thoughts like – kya muh dikhaunga ghar par!!" I answered.

'Toh fir!! Dada, dadi ne kaise react kiya tha?' he dragged himself closer, to the corner of the sofa.

"Maze ki baat toh ye hai ki unhone react hi nhi kiya. I can't remember them broaching up this incident even once, till date. And the fact that there was no social media in those days saved me from a lot of flak from relatives."

'Wow! That was smart of them. Their non-confrontational behavior must have given you strength na?'

"For sure. It did take me 2-3 days to recover from my own self-degrading narratives but I did it nevertheless."

'That's wonderful dad. Please, continue,' Ved urged.

"Yeah." Out of nowhere, a short fat lad picked up my jhola and demonstrated it to the whole class saying, "Ye kaisa bag hai!"

Before I could finish my sentence Ved switched his expression. And I knew why.

He rose to abandon me.

"Kya hua Ved?" I asked him, feigning surprise.

'Dad, please, you already know,' more than angry he looked hurt.

"No. I don't know," I said in a compassionate tone.

'You know that the term 'fat' triggers me. You know, I was bullied, harassed, at my hostel for being overweight. You already know that is one of the primary reasons I don't want to attend college for further studies. Everyone keeps ragging me everywhere.

Of all the people, I least expected you to call someone fat.'

"I am extremely sorry son. I didn't do it intentionally. Let me explain. Please sit," I said tapping twice the handrest of the sofa.

He plummeted, with a hint of skepticism.

"First things first, do you think you are fat?" I stressed over every word deliberately.

He took a minute before responding.

'Yes dad. I am.'

"That's a great start my boy. Accepting one's flaws is the very first step of handling criticism. It takes extreme courage to accept."

'Thanks, dad. However, what I am unable to perceive is - why do I boil every time someone else says it?'

"Because everytime someone else says it, you take it too personally."

'Matlab?'

"Matlab mujhe lagta hai sirf aap hi nahi aapki puri generation har chhote se comment ko personal attack ki tarah lene lagi hai. Aap logon ko lagta hai ki sabhi log aapko nicha dikhana chahte hain."

'Isn't that true? Don't they want to inject me with an inferiority complex? Don't they want me to feel insecure?

"May be, it's true. May be, you are right. The fact is no one, except the person who does it, can give you a correct answer. What I can surely say is - **no one can make you feel inferior, except you.** No matter what people say; no matter what people do; the only thing that matters is what you keep repeating to yourself inside your head."

I paused for a microsecond to let my words sink in.

"If you don't believe me, next time you get triggered, just pay attention to your thoughts, jot them down instantly, revisit them after a few days and you will know where the actual problem lies."

'Is it that easy dad?' he drew out a tired sigh.

"No, it's not easy at all, son. It will require heaps of patience, practice & perseverance but trust me, once you learn this art, you will sail through life much more smoothly. It's all in the mind, beta."

'Fair enough, dad. Sounds like a practical solution. I will certainly give it a go,' he assured me, hope lurking in his eyes.

"And by the way, I think it's high time you work on your fitness, not for people, not for aesthetics, but for your health's sake."

He considered it. 'Sure dad. I will start from tomorrow'. It won't be wrong to say I saw enthusiasm in his voice.

"That's more like my boy," I landed a little pat on his head.

There was no trace of tightness left in his posture. It seemed that the monkey was off his back. He kissed the back of my hand and requested me to go ahead with my story.

"Yeah, sure. I snapped at him, snatched my jhola, deposited it back in it's place, put my chin on top of it, looped it with my arms & closed my eyes in an attempt to avoid any eye contact whatsoever."

'Ae ladke! Idhar aa,' a growling voice passed an order.

I looked up. My eyes fell upon a small gathering of students around the 1st row of 5th column. A lean, tall guy dressed in the school uniform seated at the corner of the desk, facing me, with his left leg resting on the bench in an acute angle & his right leg hanging in the air, was staring straight into my eyes.

I inched towards him reluctantly.

'New admission?' he enquired.

"Yes," I squeaked.

'Kahan se aaya hai tu?'

"Nepal se".

'Kya!! Nepal se!! Itni dur se aaya hai toh kisi ache school mein jata. Yahan kyun aa gaya pagal,' he laughed at me as soon as his sentence ended. Within no time the whole class was laughing at me.

'Disgusting people!! I am amazed to know there was ragging in your era too!!' Ved postulated.

"It has always been there in some form or the other, son. We all find our own ways to deal with it."

'Hmm. Dad, what was the name of the school? Was it really not good? And why did you migrate in the very first place?'

"St. Thomas High School, Kolkata. It was kind of okay. I migrated.....

'Ved, Ved, why are you not picking up your phone? Come here, talk to your friend,' Ved's mom yelled from the other room.

'Oopsy!,' he cantered away saying, 'I will be back in 5 mins, don't go anywhere dad.'

My phone rang. It was Veer, my elder son.

"Hey Veer, what's up?"

He didn't reply.

"Veer, Veer, are you there?" "Kya hua beta?"

In between the sobbing, his words came out tumbling one over the other. I was unable to make sense of his rambling.

My stomach flipped.

Nonetheless, **I collected myself and did what dads do –don't show emotion, just handle the situation.**

It is in these kinds of moments, that I long for a manual, which lays down the laws of tackling a heartbroken soul.

On the other hand, as always, I knew I needed to find my own way. I rolled up my sleeve.

I decided not to disturb the air; I decided to keep my mouth shut; I decided to hold some space for him; It worked wonderfully.

He spoke; after a minute of hush.

'It's not happening dad. I am giving it my all but it's simply not happening.' His words were wobbly and unstable. I could feel his pain. It clenched my heart.

"Did they reject you again?" I pried, humanly.

Getting rejected messes up with one's confidence. And getting rejected repeatedly messes up with one's entire being; one's whole identity. Be it in whichever field of life, each of us has to face it sooner or later. Hence, we must develop our ability to digest the rejection without getting constipated. It's mandatory for our sanity.

Veer wants to be a singer. Today was his 6th attempt at cracking 'The Next Superstar' audition.

I didn't hear him respond.

"It's okay beta. Koi baat nahi," I tried to cheer him up.

He cut me mid-sentence.

'Baat hai dad. I have been training for 10 years and still can't crack it. I don't think I am good enough. You must be thinking the same, right?' he asked me in a grief-stricken voice.

I wondered straight away - **when we have self-doubts, do we actually measure ourselves on our own yardstick or someone else's yardstick?**

"No. You are wrong. I think you are working extremely hard."

'Does working hard matter, if I am not getting the results?'

"Yes. It does. It gives you satisfaction."

'Dad, please, no philosophy right now.'

"Okay son. Can I tell you a fact?"

'Yes.'

"Very few people know this, I wanted to be a professional cricketer when I was a teenager. The moment your grand-dad came to know about it, he sent me to Kolkata for better cricket training. I gave almost 15 years of my life in that pursuit. I gave it my all before I felt that's enough. I felt it's not worth anymore".

'Dad! you never told me this!!' his voice came alive.

"Because it wasn't required, Veer."

'Dad, what made you decide it wasn't worth anymore? Do you ever regret giving up? How do I decide whether I should give up or push more?' he lobbed a bundle of questions in the air.

"The very fact that my quest had started eating up my inner peace pushed me to hang my boots. No, son. I have never ever regretted giving up because I know I gave it my all. And about decisions, that's a tough one. I guess the very first thing one should do before making such life decisions is to take some time. Don't let your emotions dictate your decision making process....

'Amit, why the hell is your phone busy since half an hour?' My business colleague crashed into the lobby.

Just a second Lalit.

"Got to go son. Come home. Aaram se baith ke baat karte hain."

'All set dad. will be there at the earliest. Love you.'

"Love you too, Veer."

Lalit looked bemused as he should be. Our business is in crisis. No one at home is aware of this situation. We have a really important meeting today with investors, stakeholders and clients. I should be at my office right now. Instead, he found me lounging.

'Come on Amit. How can you be so irresponsible!?' Lalit made a face.

"I am extremely sorry Lalit. My sons needed me. I was fulfilling a father's responsibilities."

'Is everything okay?' Lalit showed his concern.

"Yeah. Yeah. Nothing to worry about. I will manage. Let's go and nail it. I am absolutely ready & prepared for the meeting."

We flew out.

CHAPTER III

First Love

कुछ गलतियाँ इतनी

हसीं होती हैं

की कर लेनी चाहिए

"Why always me? You should know about his mischief too. No matter what, I am not going this time!!" She screamed at her husband who was carrying 2 bags full of vegetables in his hands.

It was the busiest hour of the morning. The vegetable market was pulsating with people. Her rampage grabbed a lot of attention. Heads, especially male heads, spun from different directions towards the scene.

'Why didn't you tell me earlier then? I would have prepared myself,' he shot back in an attempt to salvage his prestige.

A lonnnngg glaaaaare with a few heavy breaths from her performed its magic.

'Anyways, not a big deal. Relax. I will go.'

Genius is about knowing when to step back.

'Let's hit the road. I will drop you home and gallop to school.'

The central cause of the whole fiasco you read above was their ten year old son, Rohan. A little notorious - no, not a little - he was a king of mischief. Everytime he was caught, his mom was the one who had to take all the condemnation. However, on this occasion, she was adamant to send her apathetic hubby in the parent-teacher meeting.

He parked his Activa outside the main entrance.

It was his first visit to the school in 5 years.

'May I come in Sir?' he gasped at the doorstep.

Before Sharma ji gave his permission, he sailed in, saying, 'Please don't mind, I am getting late for my job,' with a smirk on his face.

Sharma ji had a habit of rising from his chair whenever a guest walked in, as a courtesy. Not this time though. He opted to digress.

'Hello Sir, I am Rohan's father,' he extended his hand.

This was Sharma ji's moment. He ignored the waiting hand. He felt relieved. Matters were settled.

"Have a seat Mr. Pathak. Great to see you," obviously he did not mean a letter of his statement. "Mrs. Pathak didn't come this time?" he tried to conceal his disgust behind a broken smile.

'Actually, she wanted to come but I requested her, I mean, I told her, I will go this time.'

"Oh! That means. You chose it willingly. Nice to see you sharing the responsibility," the crusty Sharma ji sniggered.

'Thanks. So, what's the matter?' he questioned.

"Your son Rohan has gone a bit too far this time."

'If you don't mind, can you please get to the point sir? I have other commitments as well.'

Mr. Pathak kept sinking in his eyes.

"Yeah, sure."

He pulled out a drawer across his waist beneath the table, extracted a piece of paper and plonked it in the middle of the table with a brutal thud.

"Rohan gave it to one of his classmates the day before yesterday, after the school got over. The little girl was too flabbergasted to disclose it at home, nonetheless, she came to my office yesterday and handed it to me. I was shocked, literally shocked. This is absolutely disgusting. Intolerable stuff. Enough is enough. I think I am done with your lad. I feel the best option is to admit him to another school," his tone was as brusque as it can get.

'What is this?' Mr. Pathak was stunned. He was not prepared for this kind of onslaught.

"An application. A love application to be more precise."

'What!'

He grabbed the paper by its neck and established an eye contact with it.

Dear Shilpi,

Subject: Love

I am fine here. Hope you are fine too.

I beg to state that I really like you. From the first day I see you in school. Don't know why but everything feels good when you are near. Wanted to say this earlier, cannot do it due to lack of courage. Finally, I found some now. I also want to know what you think about me. Hope you will not get angry. Hope you will grant your permission to love you. Waiting eagerly for your reply.

Thanking you

Yours faithful

Pathak

The more he read, the paler he got. In the end, what should have been a dark red face seething in rage, turned out to be a chalk white face dripping embarrassment.

Just when he was racking his brain for suitable words, there was a knock on the door.

"May I come in Sir?" she waited calmly at the threshold.

"Yes, please," Sharma ji stood up, his disgruntled face quickly changing gears.

She walked in gracefully. Clad in a beautiful bottle green saree with a sleeveless black blouse combined with a tiny black bindi in the centre of her forehead. Black & green bangles in the ratio of 2:1 in each hand & stylish black slip-ons completed her glamorous look.

Mr. Pathak escorted her all the way from the door to the chair beside him.

"Do we know each other?" she turned to his right, diving directly into his eyes expecting him to stop his ogling.

'Not really but feels like it,' he answered coquettishly. 'Hi, I am Rohan's father. You can call me Pathak,' he informed with an extended hand.

She shook her head and turned away, now facing Sharma sir who enjoyed the insult without displaying it.

"Hello sir, I am Shilpi's mother."

"Oh! We are meeting for the very first time. Great to see you Mrs. Gupta." This time he meant every letter of his statement.

"Call me miss gupta please. And I don't think you will feel the same after knowing the motive of my visit," her words were blunt.

"But you just said you are Shilpi's mother?" Sharma ji knitted his forehead.

She glanced at the name plate kept at the corner of the table before proceeding, 'Yes, Mr. Sharma, I am. But I am not yet married. She is my adopted child.'

This statement had a startling effect on the men present. For a moment, they craved to conduct an inquiry behind her single status but they decided not to encroach into her private matters.

"Pardon, miss Gupta. Would you like some tea or coffee?" He strived to make her comfortable.

This query disappointed Mr. Pathak. And he made sure he let Mr. Sharma know about his disappointment through his furrowed brow.

Sharma ji looked into his eyes for a split second and everything was fine the next second. It was a conversation which can only happen between two males. With a female around, one male perfectly understands what the other male requires. It's a god gift, I guess.

"Nothing. Let's get the ball rolling. I would like to inform you that I have already read the love letter or should I say love application," she dragged the topic back.

"Buuuut Shilpi haaad said she didddd not tell ......," Mr. Sharma stuttered, afraid of the future.

"She is right Mr. Sharma. She didn't reveal anything. I got to know about it when I was digging out her lunch box from her school bag. I saw a crumbled piece of paper hiding in a corner. And being a girl I am well aware what these papers generally contain. I have been through it myself.'

At this point, she glanced at Mr. Pathak.

Her confronting eyes made him uncomfortable. He made an voluntary decision not to stretch the uneasiness by looking back at her.

"Anyways, I did not trouble her with my interrogation. I was determined to meet the principal and the lad's parents. Luckily, I found both of you here."

"Good thaaat you came to meeeet us," he fumbled with the words, "Please tell us what can we do for you?"

Another eye-contact from Sharma ji, demanding co-operation this time. Mr. Pathak had no other choice. He knew he was at fault. A slow blink from him gave an assurance to Sharma ji.

She took her time.

"To be honest," she began, "It should not be tolerated at all. However, there was a real childish innocence in his writing which made me smile. I found it really cute.'

She took a pause as if providing time to the listeners to chew her words.

"Sir, I request you not to take any strict action against the boy. Give him a warning and let him be. He will learn. I will handle my child."

Sharma sir looked astonished. "Are you sure Miss Gupta?" he confirmed.

"Absolutely sure."

She now turned to the other man. "And you Mr. Pathak, please keep your belongings carefully."

Mr. Pathak was bemused. He nodded in disbelief.

Sharma sir was puzzled.

'Thank you sir. I will take your leave now.'

Before he could offer a Thank you in return, she cat-walked towards the exit.

'Sir, I am getting late as well. Thank you for everything. I will leave too.' Picking up the paper from the table, he sprinted to catch her.

Sharma ji was more than happy to allow him to disappear.

'Is she ......?' Pathak needed a verification.

'Excuse me?' he called her.

She stopped right outside the entrance, near the Activa.

"You have grown old Pathak," she winked at him.

'Are you ....?'

"I am amazed that you have preserved it for so long," she cut him short.

"Hi Pathak, I am Shilpi, your Shilpi," she held out her hand.

His cheeks turned tomato-red. He took her hands into his. For a while, he forgot to let them go.

'Oh my god! I can't believe it. Such a coincidence!'

"Not a coincidence at all. The moment I saw this little girl named Shilpi in the orphanage, I knew right there, she was the one I had to adopt. How could I let another Shilpi live her life without a mom!"

He had slipped into a trance. He failed to register those words.

'How did you recognize me?' he spoke finally.

"Such a silly question. I remember everything. The moment I read it, I knew it was the same letter you had given me during our school days. How can I forget your poor handwriting!"

And they broke into a hearty laughter.

"I am still waiting for an answer, why have you preserved it for so long?" she asked after they were done with their laugh.

'Such a silly question. You were my first love, darling. How could I discard my first love letter? Who does that!'

It was her turn to blush.

"You are crazy," she declared before seizing the application from his hands. "It's not safe with you. And anyhow, it should stay with the person for whom it was meant."

He didn't protest. Like he hadn't when she had rejected his application.

'Let's go, I will drop you home,' he tried to erase the awkwardness.

"No thanks. I am alright."

'Seems like you are still very clear about what you want.'

She gave a dab on his shoulder.

'It's okay. As you wish. Bye, Take care,' he concealed his despair behind a strained smile.

"You too, Pathak."

CHAPTER IV

Behind The Curtain

किस आधार पर किए जाने चाहिए चुनाव

जहाँ चले दिमाग की नाव या जहाँ हो दिल का बहाव ?

The 24 inch LED screen hung in the middle of an extremely white wall was blaring a variety of news, unaware that the listeners were not interested. She was one of those listeners; dressed in a black kurta & faded blue jeans, sipping her coffee and gaping out of the window. A stained knife rested next to her handbag, covered with a blue silk scarf.

She plopped the empty coffee mug on the table, producing a loud noise.

'Are you alright?' enquired the guy dressed in a casual tshirt & lower.

'Yeah. No worries. Just a regular headache, I guess,' she said, rotating her index & middle finger in a circular motion on the sides of her forehead in an effort to mitigate her headache.

'Got you'. He squinted at the blue scarf, 'kaam ho gaya kya?'

'Haan'. Her voice, still groggy, 'dusra assignment kya hai?'

'I will let you know in the evening, meet me at 4:00 PM. Meanwhile, have some rest.'

'Okay. Yeah, you are right actually. I need some rest after last night's vigil. See you later then. Bye.'

She left in a haste, packing all her unfurled stuff into her purse.

The door was ajar. The big round clock above the door said, it was 4:00 p.m. She twisted her body diligently to avoid generating any sound while entering. Holding that same knife in her right hand, she lifted her bare heels, creating an arch in her feet and moved slowly towards her target.

He was sitting on a chair in the middle of an empty hall, head tilted downwards, some sheets of paper lying on his thighs, hands resting on the arms of the chair.

She was now close enough to strike a lusty blow. Raising the knife high over her head, she chanced her arm. The knife went straight into the chair's belly. He rolled on to the floor, petrified.

She had Missed!!!

He looked up at her in horror, 'Thank God!! I bowed down in time to pick up this paper. Tu pagal hai kya!! Sach mein lag jaata toh?'

'Kaash ki lag jaata, I would love to get rid of you. You know what, I am still lacking practice I think, let's do it once again,' she elbowed him playfully.

'You are crazy, man! I am not doing this play with you. I would request Sir to change my partner,' he kept the act alive.

'Hahahaha. Ok baba. I am sorry. Kitna darpok hai tu!!' she complained.

Without exhibiting any restrain, he cackled.

'Let's begin now. Yesterday night, I stayed up late to complete my first assignment. I have memorized all my dialogues, and also arranged for this stained knife. What's the second assignment?'

'Arvind sir has instructed both of us to practice together, at least for two hours, on a daily basis so that we get comfortable with each other and more importantly, we immerse ourselves into the characters so that it doesn't look fake on the stage and people connect to them easily.'

A play named 'Badla' written and directed by the veteran actor/director Arvind Khanna was to be staged in a week.

He was playing the bad guy and she was playing the part of a rape victim in the play. They were assigned the lead roles for the very first time.

She began to rehearse her lines in front of the mirror to keep track of her expressions. He settled on the floor at a distance. He peeked at her for no good reason. Her charisma was compounding on a daily basis, he thought. Every time he saw her, he fell for her head over heels. He loved her uninhibited nature, her energy, her confidence, her sense of humour, her alluring smile, her melodious tone and perhaps the most powerful quality of her- honesty.

She is undoubtedly the most beautiful thing that has ever happened to him, he thought and his face brightened.

She noticed him smiling, 'What makes you smile, you silly boy?'

He swayed his head, 'nothing.'

They had bumped into each other for the very first time around an year ago at this same place. They had landed, seeking admission in one of India's top theatre group 'AAWAZ'. Sagar had quit his corporate job to fulfill his ambition of working with 'The Arvind Khanna'. He was a huge name in theatre circles. He had trained a number of people who went on to become massive movie stars.

As far as Sagar is concerned, he had seen Arvind Sir for the very first time in Shri Ram Auditorium two years ago. A short fellow wearing a loose pant and a half-sleeved shirt, hair scattered scantily on his scalp, sporting a white beard had taken the stage after the completion of a play titled 'ek mamooli aadmi'. He introduced himeself, his actors and answered all the public queries with a smile on his face. That was the first time Sagar had felt the birth of a desire to become an actor and train under this charming man.

Once under his wings, Sagar began idolizing him, not only as a professional but also as a person. He wanted to be like him. He embraced his ethics, his values, his ideologies. He used to copy his mannerisms, his walk, his talk and what not. He used to spend most of his day around him so that he could soak up as much as possible.

Should we idolize anyone? If yes, on what grounds? And what happens if that person acts opposite to what he preaches?

Whereas Shreya had joined just for fun, just to experiment with something new in life. Later on, Sagar became the reason she never left the group. Although they hadn't made it official, yet, everyone in the group was cognizant of their brewing romance.

Enough is enough. Shreya wanted to make it official now. She wanted to propose to him without any delay. There was no way she could do it without the assistance of Arvind sir. They teamed up pretty easily. Arvind sir showed no reservations whatsoever. Today was the day. Everything was set. He had intentionally asked Sagar & Shreya to practice together. It was all part of the larger plan. Shreya was super excited.

In the middle of her rehearsal, she kept an eye on her phone. She was waiting for Arvind sir's signal. A notification cropped up. It read 'meet me at the earliest.' She was expecting something else.

She was bewildered but she obliged. Without thinking twice.

'It's an emergency Sagar. I will be back in half an hour. Continue your practice,' she spoke while haring out of the practice hall.

The number you are trying to call is not reachable.

It's been 3 hours since she left. It's 8 PM now.

There is no sign of Shreya.

She never does this!

She is extremely punctual & responsible. Sagar is worried now. His calls are not getting through. He is unable to gather any information about her from any of her friends.

He kicked the chair in frustration.

A silver colored key bobbed out onto the floor from Sagar's bag, kept on the chair.

The sound of the toppling key on the marble floor helped him remember that Shreya had given him a spare key of her flat.

Although it seemed pointless, he wanted to take every chance. He scooted to her flat in no time.

He did not find Shreya . Rather, he found a tape recorder and a note. 'The note said 'play this tape'. With his heart hammering in his chest, he pushed the play button.

'Sagar, I don't know how to begin. I am literally in a state of trauma right now so I will keep it short. I had rushed out to meet Arvind sir because he was supposed to help me plan a surprise proposal for you; but I was presented with the shock of my life. He molested me and tried to force himself upon me. Somehow I managed to flee. I have no evidence to prove it. So, I don't know if anyone will believe me. I am not sure about you either. Hence, the best thing I could do for myself was to leave everything behind and start afresh. If you trust me and want to be with me, you know where to find me. Lots of love, Shreya.'

He collapsed on his haunches; his elbows squeezing his head; fingers clasped behind the head. Every noise in the background faded. All he could hear was a long 'tang', the kind of a sound a meditation bowl emits.`

The monologue began.

Shreya never lies.

But

How

Is it possible!!

Arvind sir?

My hero? My idol?

No, he can't do this.

The fact is the moment we adore someone, we start celebrating them. We put them on a pedestal. We are unable to see them as they are at that moment. More often than not, we see their image we have projected in our mind which prohibits us from seeing their flaws, from accepting their bitter truths, from confronting them. We do everything in our capacity to defend them. And that is one of the primary reasons, we take time to come to terms with a heartbreak. Be it a romantic one or any other heartbreak.

In addition, when circumstances force us to choose between two people we adore, it gets doubly difficult. No one teaches us these subtleties of life!

If you were Sagar, who would you choose - your partner or your guru?

It was a houseful. The auditorium was packed with an anxious audience. The hype of 'Badla' was palpable. People were in, well before the scheduled time. They didn't want to miss any of this drama. The wait was over. It was going on better than expected. Actors were able to captivate the spectators by their performances. Arvind sir's daughter played Shreya's part. Sagar played his part. People cheered and whistled at various stages. A standing ovation was the proof of its success. The director of the Play, Arvind khanna, came on the stage to thank the onlookers for their love and support. As was the custom, several questions were thrown at him.

'Arvind sir, according to you, what should be the punishment for rape? or molestation for that matter?' a man in the red turban asked.

'He should be hanged till death,' Arvind sir replied promptly.

A big round of applause ensued.

CHAPTER V

Abdul Karim

किस्से, कहानियाँ और फ़साने

क्या सच, क्या झूठ, कौन ही जाने !?

He glared at me from the top of his brown rimmed glasses with his head kneeling a touch. I noticed him scanning my black colored satchel from the periphery of my eyeballs. However, I had kept my gaze absolutely straight trying to pass an impression of his stare going unnoticed. It was a typical old bag carried on the shoulder by a long strap and closed by a flap. Although none of my family member's initials was AK, these black letter stickers were pasted on the flap, one on each side. He was sitting across the road on my right, outside his crumbling house on a chair which looked as old as him. Perturbed by his steady gaze, I added speed to my already brisk walk. This was my first encounter with the uncle.

About 15 steps ahead, on my left, stood a huge building painted in baby pink which had a giant black & golden door made up of iron, quite similar to those shown in the South-Indian movies. The door had neighbours. 5 shutters on one side, a single shutter on the other side. All of them were used as godowns, opening only occasionally. The door and the shutters carried the building on their head. And all of them together prevented eyes from spying inside the premise where the construction of my new house was in progress. The other three sides were efficiently guarded by high concrete walls painted in light yellow. This was my first encounter with the new house.

I had returned to my hometown after a span of 1 year. The construction has been going on since then. I was surveying all the nitty-gritty of the new construction when my dad entered through the door shouting. Very soon I found out, it was a usual occurrence. Everytime he entered the premises, he would shout at someone or the other. Not his fault though, the workers were not easy to handle. While inspecting the freshly erected pillar, he propelled a statement towards me, 'For the next 1 month, take care of all the responsibilities of the construction'. It was neither a suggestion nor a query. It was a crystal clear statement. All I could do was nod in agreement.

From the next day, sometimes on the bike, sometimes by foot, I left my rented house at 9 a.m. sharp. Everyday, I found him sitting at the same spot, in two positions only, either with his knees bent & both feet touching the floor or one of his feet lying on the other at a 90 degree angle, gawking at me & my bag with a group of horizontal lines on his forehead. At times, it felt like he wanted to say something. But he never did.

Everyday something new about him came into my observation. One day, I noticed him parking a wad of tobacco in his mouth. One day, I noticed his white colored taqiyah (cap worn by muslims) which had two blue colored lines circling its centre; One day, I noticed his imperfect white, u shaped flowing beard trying to touch his chest; One day, I noticed his half-sleeved round necked white banyan; One day, I noticed his white spotless kurta. One day, I noticed his check-patterned lungi; One day, I noticed his black casual shoes with no laces, classic shoes worn by elderly people.

One day, when I was trying to polish my riding skills, I lost control over the bike and fell beside the sewer which was just 5 steps away from uncle's house.

Everytime we fall, we are so self-conscious about people around us. Did they watch us? What would they think about us? How would they react? What would they say?

I dusted myself. I looked around. He was still sitting at the exact same spot, watching me fall, unfazed by my condition.

Few days later, after I set foot inside the construction site and left the giant door open, I saw him walking - for the very first time in all these days. More than the walk, it was a hobble. He was hobbling to & fro before collapsing outside the building's gate. I jumped up from my chair to catch him, only to see his son arrive at the scene in a blue & green checked lungi and a brown colored banyan. The first thing he did was -scold him. He roared 'who told you to walk alone? You keep doing whatever you like. This is not tolerable at all.' To be honest, I didn't like the way he raised his voice at his father. But the only thing I could do was - be a mere spectator.

He held uncle's right shoulder softly, circled his arm around his waist and they walked away in extremely small strides.

It was the 25th day of my arrival in my hometown. I left my home at the same time I used to. Again on a motorbike. Despite the earlier accident, I had kept at it. And as they say, consistency breeds success. It was proving true for me. My control was getting better and better.

I crossed uncle's home. He was not there. His prying eyes were absent. I felt I missed them. Maybe, I had gotten used to those eyes and it's absence made me a little uneasy.

Another day passed without seeing him.

And another.

Now, I began to conjure up probable reasons for his absence. Perhaps, he is ill. Perhaps, he is not in the town. Perhaps, he has changed his timing.

I could have easily asked my maid regarding uncle's whereabouts if she was in town. She used to work in both the houses. But, she has been on a one week leave on the pretext of going to her village from the very next day uncle disappeared. I have always been intrigued by the fact that she still survives without a mobile phone in this modern age, especially for a middle-aged working woman like her who has a family to feed. There was no question of calling her.

I had to wait.

I presume, most of us are familiar with this idea - we generally dream about things that keep our mind occupied for a length of time.

One night, he hobbled into my dream. He was seated on the same old chair. Looking at me with the same glued gaze. I was walking to the premises. This time he called me, 'Son, listen.' Surprised by his unanticipated words, I stopped, turned my head clockwise, pointed a finger on my chest, squeezed my eyebrows and murmured 'me?'

'Yes, you'. He shot back.

I drifted towards him with unsure steps. He beckoned me closer. I was now standing right next to him. The air laden with the smell of freshly prepared 'beedi' sneaked into my nose. The inevitable response to it was a sneeze. 'umm... sensitive boy', he said, followed by a nasty laugh.

Days kept ticking. I had no clue what had happened to him. I wanted to know before I headed back to my hostel.

Finally, I saw him.

There he was. Flapping his hands in the water, screaming for help, making unsuccessful efforts to keep his head raised above water. After a minute or so, the flapping ceased, a pin-drop silence sprawled in the air, and the head disappeared into the water. The only thing left was ripples.

I broke into a sprint to rescue him but fell headlong. And woke up.

Another dream, it was.

Doesn't matter if someone is just an acquaintance, doesn't matter if it is just a dream, seeing someone die in your dream can really be nerve-racking. Although my body was drenched in sweat, I felt the heat. I picked up a towel from my cupboard, took a bath, dried myself up and returned to bed. Failing repeatedly to achieve any sleep.

'What does this dream mean?', 'Is uncle in trouble?', 'What should I do?' my thoughts pinballed. I kept changing my position on the bed hoping it might change the direction of my thoughts. Only after wasting an hour, sleep penetrated my eyes.

Next morning, I was hanging back. 'You have to do it, just go', my inner voice pushed me.

Conscious of my hefty steps, I tiptoed into uncle's house. It would be an understatement to say it was an old house. At least the exterior wore some paint, however aged it was. On the contrary, the interior was totally paintless. Absolutely naked. Large cobwebs decorated the ceilings and corners. Spiders of different sizes guarded those cobwebs.

I was not able to see the faces. 'Where is that black satchel?' an angry voice tore the silence.

'I have deposited it in a safe place,' in came the reply coupled with that same nasty laugh.

I raced back towards the exit before anyone could smell my presence.

As soon as I reached home, I asked my father about that black satchel.

'Dad, is this bag ours?'

'No, son. About a month ago, I found it in my scrape shop. It was in such a good condition that I wondered why would anyone throw it away as a scrape!'

'Oh! And what about the sticker A.K.?'

'I guess it should be the initials of its real owner.'

The next day, my final day in the town, I departed from the house as usual, at 9 AM. There was a large crowd outside uncle's house. Everyone was dressed in white. Everyone wore a gloomy face.

I parked my bike in a corner and asked a young lanky fellow 'What's the matter?'

Instead of using words, he chose to use gestures to answer my question. Pointing towards a banner, he mumbled, 'he is no more.'

Perhaps, it was an ancient photograph. His beard was still black. There was no sign of spectacle. His skin looked tighter. Besides the blurred photograph, a name was written in bold letters - Abdul

Karim. Just below the photograph, right across the frame, this line was punched- "Inna lillahi wa inna ilayhi raji'un" (Verily we belong to Allah, and truly to Him shall we return).

It has been my practice for long. Everytime I see a dead body, witness a funeral or attend a condolence meeting, my head automatically stoops, eyes get closed, hands make a Christian cross and my lips mutter a 'Rest in Peace'.

I was in the middle of my unconscious routine, when I overheard someone 'he left us too soon. Who will look after the old man now?'

The moment I lifted my head, I saw a shadow hobble towards me from the doorway.

His red swollen eyes met my white puzzled eyes. The way he leered at me escalated my aversion for him.

Terrorised, I bustled out of his proximity.

CHAPTER VI

Love: A Beautiful Mystery

यूँ ही कभी मिल जाना तुम

यूँ ही कभी टकराना तुम

बातों में वक़्त ज़ाया ना करना

आँखों से सब कह जाना तुम

'What is Love?' asked Raman, leaning forward, his elbows resting on the table, fingers tangled into one another.

Both of them, sitting across the table, glanced at each other for a brief second, startled.

Geet blinked her eyes signaling Gaurav to answer.

Despite the fact that their relationship was pretty young, only 6 months old, they understood these signals with ease.

Gaurav began, dragging out words from his mind, "Uncle, I think when we admire someone excessively, we are in love with them."

Emitting a long sigh, Raman drew himself back into the chair.

'And what do we admire about people?' he cross-questioned, skating his fingers along his beard knowingly.

'Could be anything Uncle. The way they look, the way they talk, the way they walk, their character, their behavior, their thoughts, their wealth, their name, their fame etc.' There was a tinge of assertiveness in these words.

Raman - a fortyish, brown-haired man smirked, 'Don't you think all these parameters are extremely volatile? Too susceptible to change?'

At this point, Geet squirmed & chose to eyeball her uncle.

If there was anyone in this world Raman loved the most, it was Geet, her niece. This love saga had began when she was barely two months old. Raman had started to 'move on' from his first breakup. It had taken him 3 months to accept whatever had occurred. Still full of questions, one fine morning, when he was lying on his back on the floor, to perform the 'Savasana', someone deposited Geet on his chest. He snapped at the person, then again, let her lie there observing the ceiling like a scientist. It did not take him long to explode into tears. He felt exactly the way he used to feel with her ex; So full of love, in his heart, in his mind. This genuine organic love overwhelmed him. And that day, he uncovered a beautiful mystery. The definition of love.

Love means just one thing - sweetness of emotion.

The fabric of this thing LOVE is always the same. Just that the design, the size, the exhibition varies as per the people we are dealing with and the kind of relationship we want to maintain.

Raman passed a frisky smile to her.

By the way, 'how did you guys meet?' he tried to cover up. Geet acknowledged this move with a loud nod, as if, congratulating him.

'I will tell you', she bounced in her seat. 'There is this application called Slowly on play store where one can send letters to any profile across the globe. You know, what's the best thing about this app?' Her excitement knew no bounds.

She didn't wait for an answer.

'It is based on the theme of letter writing. Your letters don't get delivered instantly. Depending on the location of the users and some other settings, these letters are delivered. Anyone up for a coffee?' she possessed this super power of changing the topic unceremoniously.

After collecting two 'yes', she shooted off instructing Gaurav, 'Okay then, you tell him the remaining part, I will be back in 10 mins love.' Raman identified that the use of the suffix 'love' at the end of the sentence was pretty needless. However, he checked himself from showing the dislike.

They are at Geet's house. Her parents are out of station today. Sensing this golden opportunity, Geet had come up with this plan of introducing Gaurav to her uncle-cum-best friend, Raman. She loved sharing everything with him. Their bond was exactly how Raman had imagined it to be on that discovery day. She always had high regards for his judgment & outlook. Now that she wanted to push her relationship with Gaurav in an unknown terrain i.e. marriage, she was yearning for counselling from Raman.

'Sure,' Gaurav took over the responsibilty.

'While going through the profiles, I found Geet's profile. Generally, I don't entertain profiles without pictures and bio but this time I did. Probably, because we had very few things in common and I thought it would be different, let's give it a go.'

He paused for Raman's reaction.

'Did you not see her age? Did you not know she was 6 years younger than you?

He sensed a sprinke of hostility in these words.

'I did uncle. But, somehow it did not matter.'

'Oh! I see!' Raman feigned a surprise.

Gaurav dished out a hesitant smile.

Raman spoke, disturbing the mini silence, 'You know what, I understand it completely. It can happen. When I had fallen in love for the second time, I had overlooked her age too.'

Instantly, Gaurav became comfortable, which bolstered him to dig in.

'What do you think uncle, should age gap matter?'

Raman was at it in a jiffy. 'For society, it does. I guess, any gap over 4 years is deemed inappropriate. Probably, the more the gap, the priorities tend to differ more as they find themselves at different stages of their lives. The level of perception may differ due to the difference in the exposure to different life experiences. Alignment in choices becomes hard to achieve. For me, it's different though. If two people have no reservations about their age gap, whatever the gap maybe, and their perception, choices, thoughts are in alignment more often than not, it's absolutely fine with me.'

'Wow. Uncle. You explained it so beautifully. Would you mind telling me the details of your love story?' Happens with all of us, I think. Once someone permits us inside their private room, we turn greedy. We fancy touching every memory.

Contrary to what Gaurav was expecting, as soon as Raman heard the request, he bloomed. All of a sudden, those days and nights of cravings to talk to someone about his breakup flashed before his eyes. Albeit, there were people who presented him with their shoulders, but he never found someone who would simply listen. Bereft of any praise; condemnation; judgement; suggestion; concern. In Gaurav, he saw a bright prospect.

He began in a hushed tone, 'I am going to keep it short though because Geet absolutely hates her. She believes I am not marrying only because of that lady, which is, of course, true by the way.'

'Oh! as you wish uncle,' said Gaurav, trying his best not to stampede any of uncle's emotions.

'She stormed in. She loved. She left,' Raman reminisced in a heavier voice, his face making an effort to conceal the grim expression.

'Without any reason?'

'Here it is.' 3 cups of coffee got placed on the centre table along with a bowl of roasted peanuts and fox nuts mixed together. 'What were you guys talking about?'

Gaurav cleared his throat, 'nothing, just about us.'

She took her seat beside Gaurav, a bit too close for Raman's liking.

'Chachu, I also need to ask you something. It's been bothering me for a while,' she said while popping a piece of peanut.

'Accchhhha. Tujhe kabse mere permission ki jarurat padne lag gayi,' Raman stretched the first word slightly.

'Hehe. Nahi bas. Acha ye batao fir. How long should one stay in the relationship before deciding to get married?'

Geet, invariably, was an extrovert. If in the zone, she could talk endlessly. She could ask bold questions, catching you wrong-footed. Although he had an inkling about the purpose of this meeting, however, he was not expecting her to mete out this doubt so blatantly.

Raman slurped his coffee, 'Beta, aisa koi bhi fix rule nahi hai. I think if you know yourself properly, as in, what ticks you on, what ticks you off, how do you react in certain situations, that's a good base to enter in a romantic relationship, and then, when you feel you are absolutely ready to share this beautiful life & it's experiences with another human being, by ready I mean you are ready to shed a large part of you for someone else's happiness, just go for it, despite the fact, that it's been only a month or 5 years. It doesn't matter, really. There is no right time. There is no way you can know anyone totally, not your own self as well, because we are an exceptionally inflammable being, hence, I would suggest just make up your mind and dive in.'

'And what if we regret later about the decision taken? For whatever reason?' Gaurav added.

Raman scratched the back of his head, 'that is always a possibility, guys. You can start disliking a person. You can start liking another person. You might not like your in-laws. You might feel tired of the effort it takes to maintain a relationship. There can be infinite reasons. The only thing that keeps any relationship intact is 'commitment'.

They peeped at each other before bowing down simultaneously for a salute.

A laughing riot accompanied.

'Chachu, we got to go now. We are getting late for our dinner date.'

Raman thought he saw a bit of a red on her cheeks.

'Oh! yes,' Gaurav reiterated. 'We will take your leave, uncle. It was a pleasure meeting you. Hope you felt the same,' Gaurav stated cheekily.

Raman didn't bother to reply.

She followed Gaurav to the door. Just before crossing the door, she halted, spun around.

Raman was standing right behind her.

She raised her eyebrows at Raman. He knew what she was seeking.

Raman gave her a slow nod.

She was all smiles. She hared off whispering a 'love you chachu.'

He smiled. Shook his head. Shut the door.

CHAPTER VII

A Life Unnoticed

ये बताओ, तुम ऐसी क्यों हो माँ

बदतमीज़ी क्यों सह जाती हो माँ !!

टोक दिया करो जब तुम्हारा दिल दुखता है

लाड़ में तुम मेरे, चुप क्यों रह जाती हो माँ !!

"Who is the patient?" Dr. Joshi, the family doctor, probed.

'My maid, Pratima. She is more like a family member though. She has been working in my house for almost 35 years now'. The latter part of the sentence was coated with a thin layer of smug.

I was sitting on the floor with my left leg bent from my knees, it's sole meeting the vertically outstretched right knee.

"Ritu ji, it will be difficult to judge without seeing the patient, can you please, at least, send me some pictures of her foot, so that I can assess the condition better?" Dr. Joshi pleaded.

'Umm... Doctor, I am not sure if I know how to do it, is it possible for you to guide me over this call?' Ritu bhabhi made a request.

"Why not! It's easy. First of all, open your whatsapp account," he paused for her to complete the first move.

'But how!! I can easily open my whatsapp account when my phone is not in any other use, but, how to do it when I am already on a call?' bhabhi sounded perplexed.

Nitin passing by caught her sight.

'Beta, idhar aana. Please help me,' bhabhi beckoned him.

"Ab kya hua yr!" Nitin plodded back rubbing his drowsy eyes.

'I need to open my whatsapp account, help me out,' she said in a slurred speech.

"Are! Kal hi toh bataya tha aapko. Why can't you remember such a small thing!?"an upset Nitin reproached.

'Nahi. Nahi. I do remember it. What I want to know is - how to do it while being on a call?' she clarified.

He shook his head, 'You are hopeless mom. Ratta mat maara kro, 50 baar kaha hai.' Dhyan se dekho ab. It's not difficult mom, just press the back button or the multiple window button and you are good to go.

'The ones at the bottom, right?'

"Yes. Absolutely right."

She beamed knowing she got it right.

'Okay. Thanks. I will do it.'

Nitin returned after 5 minutes. He saw her mother still grappling with it. He reached out for the phone.

"Give it to me, no point instructing you, I know, aapse nahi hoga," he said.

An ungainly smile escaped her lips.

Ritu bhabhi shouted while cutting the vegetables, 'Nitin, homework hua khatam?'

The 3 year old Nitin didn't reply.

She scrambled to find out the matter.

'What happened Nitin? Why have you not started yet?'

"Mom, I forgot how to hold this pencil!" Nitin exclaimed as if it was the most difficult task in the world.

She smiled. 'Kal hi toh sikhaya tha maine.' She looked at his innocent face and said, 'Koi baat nahi, dubara sikhati hoon.'

"No mom, I don't think I can do this," he objected.

'Never say that, my boy. You can do absolutely anything. Here, come, sit with me. Hold the neck of this pencil from the left side using your right thumb, from the right side using your index finger and let the pencil rest on the middle finger for the support."

He did it in his 3rd attempt.

'See. Easy peasy. No matter how many times you forget, your mom will always be there to assist you.'

Nitin sent the image within seconds; tossed the phone in the air expelling a grunt before leaving.

"Nothing to worry Ritu ji, these rashes are quite common during the summer season, apply any anti-fungal cream, that should work," replied doctor Joshi.

'Oh! Really! Thanks.'

"My pleasure. Please, don't hesitate to get back to me if I am needed."

'Sure. I will.'

"Thenku bhabhi," I showed my appreciation as soon as the call ended.

'Are! Thenku nahi. Thank you hota hai Pratima,' she corrected me.

"Oh! haan. Thank you bhabhi. Thank you for everything. Aapka ye English mein baat krne ka idea bahut kaam kr rha," with every word my facial expression changed, expressing gratitude & affection.

'You are most welcome Pratima,' she posted two back 2 back pats on my back.

"But bhabhi, I never asked you this, how did you learn English? Kitna padhi ho aap?" I asked while lifting my overweight body. I was getting late.

'10th. I was the first girl in my family to complete class 10,' her eyes gleamed, 'aur baaki Nitin ko padhate padhate sikh liya thoda. Mujhe na, bahut saukh tha English sikhne ka aur driving sikhne ka. I somehow managed to learn English but driving sikhna abhi bhi baaki hai.'

"Mummy, I have invited my boss for dinner tonight, as Pratima didi is on leave today, will you cook the food or I should order from outside?" questioned Nitin.

"Bhabhi, I am leaving. See you tomorrow," I said while moving towards the door.

She gave me a nod.

'No problem, son. I will cook,' I overheard her.

'What have you done mum!!? I told you to make paneer butter masala and you have made matar paneer!! Allergy hai unko matar se. What will he eat now!!?' Nitin said it so loudly, his boss heard it all.

He probably felt responsible for this altercation, hence, he agreed to eat whatever was available.

Once he left, Nitin blasted her again, "How can you make such a big blunder! I wish Shruti was here today."

Till now, bhabhi had listened to everything patiently but the mention of Shruti, her daughter-in-law, who was in her marital home right now, hurt her immensely. Her face turned long. She left the scene immediately, went to her bedroom and shut the door violently.

Usually, bhabhi is extremely calm & composed.

Usually, she has this set routine since bhaia's demise last year. She would wake up between 6-7 AM. Rub both her palms for a second or two, place them on her eyes. Recite some mantras before putting her foot on the floor. Touch the floor with her right hand, then, unload herself from the bed onto the floor. Freshen up. Go for a light walk, inside the house compound only. Come back. Sit on the bed again. Do a few yoga asanas. Again recite some mantras. Have a cup of bed-tea alongwith 4 biscuits. Then, her best part of the day. Reading the newspaper. Yes. On days when the newspaper was not available, she would just stare into space while ruminating, until I gave her a bucket of lukewarm water to take a bath.

As both Nitin & Shruti were working professionals, after bhaia's demise, they had recruited me to stay all day to take care of bhabhi and do all the needed chores as well. I used to come twice in a day for work. Once in the morning for cleaning the utensils and cleaning the house. Once again in the evening for cleaning the utensils.

After the bath, she would have a long stint of puja path. And when I say long, I mean it. Because, it was never less than 2 hrs, if anything, may be more on some occasions. Followed by a brunch. Followed by a tea alongwith some tv. Then, a small power nap. After she woke up, either we talked or she turned to tv again.

There were times when I would ask her, if she ever missed bhaia.

She would say yes. Almost daily. A number of times. I feel I don't have anyone to talk to, except you, of course. In the morning, I barely meet Nitin & Shruti before they are about to leave for their office. By the time they come back, I am already on my bed. So, yes, I miss your bhaia a lot. Especially when I want to talk.

I remember asking her once if she ever gets angry with the way she is treated by her kids. She had said, 'Sometimes. It's not that they abuse me or beat me up but, you know, it's just those little things when you crave for your closed one's presence, when you crave for a conversation with them, when you crave for their tender touches etc. But what can I do!? I have no one else to fall back upon, except of course, my sister who lives in another town but she has her own family and I don't want to disturb her, so, it's kind of okay. Itne bhi bure nhi hain bacchhe.'

To be honest, there are moments when I wonder what is she alive for? She is already 70 years of age.

I don't see any zest in her.

I don't see any purpose which pushes her to leave her bed every morning.

I don't see anyone showing her that kind of affection which tells you, you are important.

It's the same monotonous daily routine!!

What does the old generation live for? Or purpose is just a myth? Are we here just to live?

She would then ask for one more cup of tea, and some snacks, occasionally. Followed by her evening puja path, while I prepared the dinner. She had always believed in early dinners. She would be on her bed by 7 PM. Although, I am not sure, she sleeps before 8-9 PM. I leave the house after Nitin & Shruti arrive at 8 PM.

Today, when bhabhi was telling me about yesterday's squabble, Nitin emerged, with a bucket of warm water.

"Mummy, here it is, your bucket of water," Nitin plopped the bucket on the floor in front of her and took a seat alongside her on the bed.

When you have seen someone grow up right from his birth, you get an idea about them. I could sense Nitin's desire to give her a warm hug right there but he didn't. Instead, he did it in his mind I guess, and in reality, gave her a warm smile.

Silence hung in the air for a while. Bhabhi was clearly upset. Not in the mood to talk to him.

He grabbed her left elbow, pulled it towards himself and whispered softly, "I am extremely sorry maa. It won't happen again."

She egged him to speak louder using hand signals.

"Sorry sorry. How can I forget! Your hearing issues," he raised his voice this time, "I am extremely sorry maa. It won't happen again."

She considered it for a few seconds.

'But you have said it 20 times before as well,' she responded with an expressionless face.

"I know. Just forgive me this time. I assure you I won't repeat it. If I do, you can do whatever you like," requested Nitin.

'Sure?'

"100%"

'Ok then,' she took his hand in hers and planted a soft kiss at the back of his palm.

'Get ready mom, we will be going to the ENT doctor for your ear checkup.'

'And your office?'

"I have taken a half day. I will go to office after lunch time. First & foremost, let's address your hearing issue."

'Cool,' she said before disappearing with the bucket. She had been learning these terms to fit into her kid's world.

Upon his return from the doctor's visit, she was absolutely boiling.

'Pratima, ye le mera phone, ticket book kr mera. Yahan nahi rehna ab mujhe,' she said in a trembling voice.

'What happened bhabhi, batao?' I demanded.

'Just do as I say. Don't poke your nose into everything,' she growled.

"Bhabhi, date?"

'Aaj ki hi. Ek ghante baad hai ek train. Usme krde.'

While I booked the ticket, she packed her bag.

'You know what, I eavesdropped Nitin while he was talking to the doctor in private. He was saying - Sir, is there any point in wasting the money on a new expensive hearing device at this age? Just give her some multi-vitamins and tell her she is alright. I will be grateful to you. So, I ran away from there without informing anyone,' she disclosed the cause on her own, in one breath.

"Oh! bhabhi, it's done."

'Thanks Pratima. I will miss you.'

"When will you return bhabhi?" I was genuinely concerned.

'Don't know. Right now, all I can say is I must get away from here, for sometime at least. I will think about my future once I cool off.'

"Yes bhabhi. Take your time."

'I will. And you, don't you dare to tell anyone where I am going.'

'Ok bhabhi.'

She dragged her suitcase and herself out of the house before she could change her mind.

CHAPTER VIII

The Red Chair

तेरी तलब

सुबह की नींद जैसी है

कभी पूरी ही नहीं होती

'Are you alone?' questioned John with raised eyebrows.

"Yes," the woman answered without sounding resentful.

'Madam, don't you know today is Valentine's Day? I can't provide you with a single seat today. Either, bring another person with you or I am sorry, your ticket will be refunded,' John did his best to be as polite as possible.

"In that case, you shouldn't be selling single tickets na?" the lady made a valid point.

'Actually, we have been providing 50% discount on couple tickets on Valentine's day for 3 years now & till date, I have never witnessed a 'single' person show up on this day, hence, we were not mindful of this glitch. I agree. It's our fault but I can't help it madam. Please, try to understand. I don't have the powers to bend the rules,' John tried to convince her.

While John came up with this request, she resolved to scan the theatre for any empty seats.

A cinema hall on a Valentine's Day is a sight to behold. Couples of all ages, colors, shapes and sizes are on display. New couples struggling to keep the conversation going; Innocent couples talking with ease; Smart couples looking for an opportunity to cuddle; Naughty couples waiting for the lights to go off.

She didn't find too many empty spots barring a couple of adjacent empty seats. At that particular moment, she spotted a vacant *red chair* right at the centre of the seating arrangement. Except for this seat, all the other seats were well cushioned and well draped. Realizing the odd appearance & status of this seat, she took a chance.

"What about that seat over there, the centre one, why is it so non-identical & vacant?" she pointed her finger towards the seat.

'Mam, that is how all the seats here looked like before the renovation. And no one is allowed to occupy that seat. The owner of this theatre is rigid on that thing,' John revealed.

"In that case, can you please do me a favour?"

'As in?'

"Please, talk to your owner once. It's a humble request. Please, ask him, for an old lady's sake."

I don't think she was as old as she was pretending to be. Still, her humble demeanor forced John to give it a shot.

'Sir, there is this old lady viewer who is all alone, requesting me to allow her to occupy *the red chair*. What should I do?' John waited for the reply Mr. Andrew, the owner.

Before the reply could hit, she took the matter in her hands.

"Hello sir, it's been a long haul since I have watched any romantic movie, that too, in this prestigious movie theatre of Goa. Please, don't disappoint me. Please. If you wish, I will pay you extra ....

'No no. It's absolutely fine. Please enjoy the movie,' in came the response, cutting the lady's sentence midway.

"Thank you so much."

She handed over the phone to John.

It would be safe to say John was nonplussed. In his 10 years of service, no matter what, Mr. Andrew had never ever permitted anyone to occupy that chair. And today, he did it without any fuss!

The lady was pleased though. John showed her the way.

Watching a movie inside a cinema hall is such an enthralling experience. And most of this experience depends largely upon the projector, sound and lighting. In 1980s, Digital Light Processing projectors were used, then came LCD projectors and now it's the Laser projector which provides an ultimate viewing experience. The pitch black atmosphere created inside the hall enables one to focus on the screen religiously, which is something difficult to create at home. Also, there is no match for the theatre's sound quality.

Suddenly, the lights went off. The hall which was dazzling with bright lights moments ago, turned into a dark cave. A small 2*2 window vomited a cluster of light onto the 50 ft wide & 25 ft tall screen. The screen came to life with a roar.

It was the kind of a movie which took its time to peak. After an hour or so, the first big twist sprang up which drove the lady into her flashback.

The mature dvd player kept in Mr. Andrew's office came to life out of the blue. He was forced to remove his gaze from the CCTV screen. As it should be, the dvd player, now, was receiving all his attention. Andrew could see everything that the lady was thinking.

I found myself standing alone at the altar, my heart racing in my chest. My father stood next to me, his serious eyes locked on the elaborate entrance, waiting for Matthew to show up at any moment. Two years ago, I had envisioned this day – the peak of my love story with this guy. We met in college, and right away, there was a strong and profound connection between us. He was everything I had ever dreamed of: caring, loyal and deeply in love with me. My engagement had come about quickly, and now, with family and friends all around me, I was filled with a deep sense of joy and excitement.

As the minutes passed and he still didn't show up, a sense of unease began to creep in. Having people around, only made my anxiety worse. Tears began to roll down my cheeks incessantly. He never came.

Lights blew up announcing the interval.

With the re-introduction of lights, the dvd player blacked out.

Andrew has always been a movie buff. This dvd player was a present given to him by his one and only girlfriend. At first, he used to watch movies in it frequently. But, as the era of dvds trailed off, it turned into a mere show-piece item.

Andrew was perplexed & shocked with what had just transpired. Trying to make some sense of it all. He decided to splash some cold water on his eyes.

Generally, in the interval, people rush off for the washroom and refreshment, but not today. Not many were bothered to fuel themselves; Not many were eager to leave their partner's clutched hands; Not many heads were visible above the seats; Some were resting on the shoulder of their partner, some on the lap, some on the chest. The sudden onslaught of the lights must have ruined some potential kisses as well.

The movie resumed.

The red chair was relinquished.

In search of a better viewing angle, someone else occupied the empty chair sneakily, leaving his friend on his own.

The dvd player showed nothing this time, until the man jumped into his flashback.

I was all beefed up to go to the church. Then I received a call from my hometown. It said my parents had met with a life-threatening accident and I needed to be there at the earliest. As soon as I got the details, my phone's battery died. I was dying to inform Maria but I could not.

Although I tried my best, I could not make it in time. My parents had left the world leaving behind a frightening void.

I was completely shattered. I went into my cocoon. Avoided any contact with anyone. None of my friends knew my location and my condition. I had blocked all of them except Maria. I functioned like a zombie, unaware of what I was eating, what I was saying, what I was doing for the next few days.

As if, all this was not enough, one day, I received a message from Maria - Don't ever contact me. You are the world's worst person. Don't ever show me your face. I hate you the most in this world.

The person I needed the most in this time of distress had abandoned me. I wanted to connect to her. I wanted to clarify things. But, I did not have the courage. I was her culprit. She had all the right in the world to hate me.

The dvd player blacked out once again.

The 45 year old owner felt his eyes filling with tears.

He recalled the last time he had met his girlfriend, 15 years ago, on this same day. She had occupied that same red chair. While bidding an emotional goodbye, she had handed over a dvd player to Andrew. Her father never liked Andrew because he did not earn much. He was a small priest at that time. The first thing Andrew did after earning enough money was buy this movie theatre where he had met his beloved for the last time, renovate it, without touching 'the' sacred red chair, put in all the hard yards to become one of the richest persons of Goa.

The siren denoting the end of the show brought him back to his senses. The very first thing he did was - make a phone call to the security guards to confirm whether anyone had left the theatre.

'No sir, no one has left,' the guard informed.

The next thing he did was – he ordered John not to let anyone exit from the screening before he arrived.

The gates were closed.

'Please, bear with me, ladies & gentleman. It's urgent,' he made an announcement on the mic to pacify the restless and confused audience.

A spot light now circled the man seated on the red chair.

Andrew enquired, 'hey there, are you Matthew?'

'Yes.'

'The one who was supposed to marry Maria?'

'Yes.'

'Are you married now?'

'No, but why are you asking all this?'

'Because I am Andrew, the priest who was supposed to officiate that wedding. That was a life-changing incident for me. That day, 20 years ago, I decided, I don't want to do this anymore. And look, where I am today. I owe you guys. I will be glad if I could make a difference in your lives. Guess what, I have a good news for you.'

'What good news?'

'I suspect Maria is here too.'

'What!' Matthew jumped up in excitement.

'Yes. Please wait.'

'Maria, can you hear me? I know you can. Please head to screen 1 asap. I have a surprise for you,' the powerful speakers announced.

Within minutes, Maria appeared.

Matthew charged in her direction. She was standing right in front of the screen, exactly at the centre. With his heart pounding vigorously, he reached. Neither of them moved for the next minute.

Pouring all his pain and affection in his words, he spoke, 'I am extremely sorry Mary. Will you be able to forgive me? ever?'

'No. Never. It's not okay at all,' she replied, her tone heavy with emotion. 'I will never ever forgive you, not for disappearing. But, for, not telling me about your parents, for not sharing your grief with me. How could you do that?'

She didn't wish for an answer. She longed for his touch; a kiss on the forehead; a peck on the cheeks; a bite on her lips; a profound hug; or anything else she wasn't conscious of.

Words have their own limitations. Deep wounds require action to heal.

He hugged her. Deeply. Passionately. As tightly as he could. Her chin pressed against his shoulder. His hands wandered freely on her back.

Tears trickled down his face in random directions, 'My darling, I wanted to tell you, but... I ....

She pulled her head back and kissed his tears one by one.

'You know what, I tried extremely hard, but I could never stop loving you,' she whispered in his ear.

Taking a plunge into his eyes, she rolled out the most important question, 'Matthew, will you marry me?'

CHAPTER IX

Waiting Room

आख़री बार कब मुस्कुराए थे तुम

आख़री बार कब गुनगुनाए थे तुम ??

अपने ख्यालों का सामना, कब किया था आख़री बार

आख़री बार खुद से कब घबराए थे तुम ??

Me, mamaji, mamiji and her brother-in-law had landed here at Ruben hospital, Patna, yesterday night for my mamaji's treatment on a relative's suggestion. The hospital looked ancient. The exterior walls were painted yellow. Interior walls were all white. The structure of the building seemed totally unplanned. A doubt bubbled up in my mind regarding the efficiency of this hospital. That said, this hospital was suggested by a relative who held it in high regard. And we humans always have a tendency to follow a tried & tested method. So, here we are.

Although mamaji was not that serious, we admitted him directly into the Intensive Care Unit as instructed by the relative so that he gets better care and attention. We found ourselves, a hotel nearby, to spend the night.

<u>Day 1</u>

"What the hell! That's my seat!" the middle-aged man hustled in my direction pointing his fingers at the black slippers placed right beneath that seat I was trying to capture.

'Oh! I am extremely sorry! I didn't know depositing your slippers is a way to book your seat.' It was more of a taunt rather than an apology.

"Don't try to be smart, this is how it works here," the man barked at my face.

My companion, Pradeep uncle, who was getting utterly bored till now decided to have some fun, 'O hello! Mind your words. This is not a bus or a train. Placing your slippers means nothing.'

2 sturdy young men, his acquaintances, with broad shoulders dived in his support.

Why do we support our loved ones even when they are at fault?

People who were either standing or walking in the aisle outside the room because there were no seats available inside, quickly jumped into our support, spilling out all their frustration on the middle-aged man and his supporters.

Why do we always wait for someone to take the initiative to protest against the wrong?

It required the intervention of the security guard to stop the mayhem.

It was 9 AM. It was time for the kidney specialist, Dr. Hans. to take his daily round.

"Mr. Raju's attendant please come to room no. 224," howled a speaker in the waiting room.

Hospital had a rule. Only one person was allowed to meet the doctor or the patient at one time.

Pradeep uncle was the automatic choice because he was sent in as the decision-maker.

The moment he came back, we bombarded him with queries.

He told us - some tests were conducted last night and there is nothing serious right now. Just that the kidneys have stopped functioning altogether and the latest thing is creatinine level is beyond 10 & the heamoglobin level is 5. They will keep him under observation for a day or two and see if the haemoglobin levels rise up so that the dialysis could be done.

'Dialysis?' She frowned. I guess mamiji had never heard about it.

'Yes. Not a big deal nowadays. There is this machine which is attached to a patient's body with wires and cables that performs the function of the kidneys. There are 2 ways to do it, either through a catheter or through an AV fistula. They have opted for a catheter as fistula formation takes time. A tube will be inserted into a vein in the neck to draw the blood from the body and sent through that machine that filters it. The filtered blood is then returned to the body. That's it. Nothing to worry about.'

Some people have this knack of breaking frightening news in a way that does not seem frightening at all. Uncle surely possessed it.

'Exactly, and I believe, keeping in mind the scarcity of chairs in this room, there is no point for all of us to stay here.' I volunteered, 'I will stay till evening in case they call us again.'

Giving me a thumbs up, they took an exit from the room.

Located on the right hand side, at around 15-20 steps from the main entrance of the hospital, the waiting room was neither small nor huge, something in between. Standing at the entrance, I surveyed the whole room. On my left, sets of 3 adjoining chrome colored waiting chairs which had tiny holes in their back rest were placed in 4 rows & 2 columns, leaving approximately 1 foot gap between the 2 columns. All facing the white colored wall which had a small toilet in it's corner. On my right, just 1 set of 3 adjoining chrome colored waiting chairs were placed in an L shape. Their backrest touching the walls with pride. The remaining land on my right side, in front of the chairs, besides the toilet, was occupied by a family. A blue colored bed sheet was rolled out on the floor. Adult males were lying in obnoxious positions, revealing their innerwears, crowding on one another. Kids were looking down into the mobile phones. An old man with a long white beard was towering over them overlooking them all.

Recognizing the fact that it was not sensible to block the gate for too long, I moved ahead slightly. The speaker yelled again, not my patient's name though. I tried to locate the speaker.

The only way you could hear the announcements was through this speaker. I pondered about the small ugly black speaker ingrained into the ceiling. It was the lifeline of this waiting room.

What if this speaker malfunctions? Do they have any alternatives?

These are the kinds of stuff I do, when I am absolutely free. I look around. I think. I question.

I waited all day long. There was no announcement for Mr. Raju's attendant.

<u>Day 2</u>

Everyone woke up late except me.

I have always been a responsible chap; I also have a lot of questions; I am extremely energetic too. Perhaps, that's why I was elected to be a part of this entourage at 20 years of age.

Asking them to hurry up so that we don't miss the announcement, I left the hotel alone.

The only seat that was empty in the waiting room was the one next to a young man immersed into a fat novel.

I wondered what kind of a person this lad was? Who reads novels these days!

I surveyed the room once again. The only person who looked at ease in the entire room was that young man.

"Mr. Raju's attendant please come to room no. 224".

I was the only one available right now so I dashed out of the waiting room. About 20 feet ahead, in the opposite direction of the hospital's main entrance, I found a staircase guarded by an iron grill which was again guarded by 2 security guards, one man & one woman, both dressed in a sky blue uniform, a navy blue sweater on top which had their names written in bold letters around the chest area and a navy blue cap.

"Kahan jana hai?" The man with the trimmed moustache threw up his hand to stop me.

'Upar. Announcement hua hai abhi. Bulaya hai mujhe,' I answered.

"Attendant ho?"

'Ji'.

"Card kahan hai tumhara?" the woman joined in.

'Kaisa card?'

"Attendant card?"

'Card mere uncle ke pass hai. Wo abhi hain nahi yahan par.'

"Acha thik hai. Is baar jane dete hain. Agli baar se bina card ke nahi jaane denge."

'Okay. Thankyou.'

There was a spring in my strides. I climbed 2 stairs at once while rewinding the whole conversation in my head. I was offended by the word 'tumhara'. Shouldn't she be referring to me as 'sir' or 'aap' at least, I quizzed myself. Umar mein badi hai toh kya hua, status mein toh choti hai!!

When I reached the second floor I was stopped by a guard, again, in a similar uniform. He asked me to either remove my shoes or wear a green colored shoe cover kept inside a nearby box before entering the premises.

'kya natak hai yaar!' I poured my simmering frustration on him.

"I can't help it sir, this is my job," he replied.

'It's okay,' I toned down.

He begged me to wait outside the room along with the other people. I waited until a nurse made an appearance from room no.224 in a long white coat with a writing pad in her hand.

'Mr. Raju's attendant?'

I raised my hand. She allowed me inside a huge hall containing at least 15 beds if not more. Dr. Hans was attending each one of them hastily. The attendants and caretakers were swallowing his instructions with utmost focus. It was my turn now. Crossing my arms, I listened to him with a look of intent on my face.

"The haemoglobin levels are okay today, if it remains steady tomorrow morning as well, we will start dialysis tomorrow. We will require the attendant's consent so, please send someone older tomorrow who can make the decision," Dr. Hans declared.

When I returned back to the waiting room, I found my companions seated with a smile plastered on their face. Perhaps, it was the joy of securing 2 seats amidst a big crowd. Before I could smile back, a lady in the saree began wailing.

"Abhi umar hi kya hai us bachhe ki," she kept repeating to another lady beside her with every howl. A kid circled her waist. Fear, visible clearly in his eyes. An elderly uncle patted her head saying, 'honi ko kaun taal sakta hai beta!' The howl grew louder.

It was exceedingly difficult to witness their grief.

Is there a right age to die? Are we ever prepared to let go of our loved ones?

<u>Day 3</u>

Uncle gave his consent and the dialysis began.

He told us that mamaji wanted to meet mamiji.

'I will go today during the visiting hours,' she spoke.

Today was different. There were plenty of empty seats. We were all sitting and waiting. The middle-aged man was absent from the room today. That's the first thing I do now. I look for him the moment I enter the room. I despised him after what had transpired on the first day. I didn't want to be in his vicinity. I know it was a small incident but that's how I am. Once you are rough to me, I label you as rough.

I was lost in my thoughts when I heard that voice again, 'Can I sit beside you?'

I wish I would have said a NO. But I couldn't.

Not gonna lie, though, I made a serious effort to avoid him. I fixed my gaze on the wall in front of me until he dropped a wily "Sorry" at me.

Unable to process what just happened, I blurted out 'What?'

"I am extremely sorry for that day. It was my fault. I was tense as hell due to my father's illness and unfortunately I spilled it out on you."

'It's perfectly fine,' I replied back after gathering myself.

Is it possible for us to forgive someone without receiving their apology?

'How is your father now?' I investigated not to keep the conversation alive but I genuinely wanted to know.

"He is out of danger right now. On the other hand, according to Dr. Hans, it's better that he stays with the family for the remainder of his life."

"Remainder of his life matlab?' I could not suppress my curiosity.

"Matlab, there is no cure for his illness. It has got to a point where the medical community is helpless. It was difficult initially but now I have accepted the fact that the medical community cannot extend his life beyond a certain point."

'Why don't you try another hospital? Another doctor?' I suggested.

"We have already done that. We have consulted foreign doctors as well. No one has an answer. We brought him here because I was in denial. I was not willing to accept his death. But something inside me has shifted after my father whispered, 'I don't want to die on a hospital bed' in my ear earlier today. He is out of immediate danger now. It's better we keep him in a healthy & happy environment during his last days, so we got him discharged. Waiting here for the billing procedures to get completed."

Why is it so difficult to accept death when it's the only certain thing in our life? How long should we stretch our loved one's lives, especially, if they are not in a state to decide for themselves?

The clock struck 3.

'Let's go to meet him,' Mamiji gave me a nudge.

Mamiji was pretty docile and naïve from the outside world. Like the ladies from the previous generation used to be. I assume she was sent more for emotional support rather than anything else.

'2 people are not allowed mamiji,' I said.

'Aise kaise nhi jane dega,' she roared. Her demeanour surprised me.

'Patient se milne jana hai,' I said to the same woman guard.

"Koi ek jaa sakta hai," she growled at us.

'kyun? Milne hi toh jaa rahe hain. Dono ko milna hai,' Mamiji pulled out a flag of protest.

"Baat ko samajhie madam, aur bhi log hain milne wale, aise 2-4 log ko ek baar mein jane denge toh bahut bheed ho jaegi upar.'

'Wo mujhe nahi pata. Hum dono jaenge,' Mamiji demanded.

"Okay, wait. Let me ask upstairs".

She used an old black landline phone kept on a wooden stand attached to the wall behind her.

"Sorry sir. Only one person can go. Aap samjhaie madam ko," she implored me.

'It's okay Shaanti ji. She will go,' I announced with a reassuring smile.

"Thankyou for understanding sir," she smiled back.

<u>Day 4</u>

My phone number was registered in the hospital as the attendant's number. I received a call from the hospital early this morning to arrive in the waiting room as soon as possible.

"Sabhi log is waiting room ko khaali kar dein," ordered the man with the mop.

'Can you please wait for 5 minutes. We need to offer our Namaz,' requested the old man with a long white beard falling on his chest.

It was the same old man I had seen on the very first day with his family.

'No. I cannot wait. I need to perform other duties as well,' the lanky man raised his voice.

'5 minute mein aisa kuch nhi bigad jaega,' a man in a turban raced in the old man's support.

I was witnessing the scene from closeby. I jumped from my seat as well, to boost the support. Albeit, there were only a handful of people in the morning, we swelled into a group rapidly.

He gave in.

The old man gaped at us, his eyes oozing appreciation.

'Mr. Raju's attendant, please come to room no. 124,' the speaker screamed.

I thought the announcer had made a mistake. I rushed to room no. 224 where I came to know I was at fault. He had been transferred to room no. 124 which was a HDU – high dependency unit. I found myself standing in the queue once again accompanied this time by a girl of my age.

"Dr. hans?" she enquired perhaps sensing my worry.

'Yes,' I replied.

"Don't worry, he is a fantastic doctor. He has been treating my grandfather for 20 years."

'Oh! Okay. If you don't mind, can I ask you something?' I filed a petition.

"Umm. Yeah. Sure," she agreed.

'My patient has been transferred from ICU to HDU. Does that mean he is in a better condition or worse condition?'

I could sense her, smiling at my innocence.

"It is neither of them I suppose. It's because they have better dialysis infrastructure in this room."

'Oh! I see'.

"Your patient hasn't eaten anything since morning, please help," the ward boy appeared, threw the statement at me and disappeared.

I wheeled in. He was lying on the bed on his back. He took a glimpse of me from the corner of his eye. I observed him for a second. Mamaji looked leaner; fragile. A catheter (a flexible tube) was attached to his neck. It looked tremendously painful. I gritted my teeth together.

'Kya hua mamaji, khaa kyun nhi rhe?' I held him by his elbow attempting to lift his upper body and make him sit.

'3 din se sirf daliya, khichdi khaa rhe hain, man nahi hai ab ye khane ka,' he complained like a child.

'Arey! Ek do din ka baat aur hai. Discharge hone ke baad jo khana hai khaaiega,' I tried to soothe him.

'No'. He was adamant.

'Thora sa kha lijie. Hum khilate hain,' Sitting alongside, I took the plate in my hands.

It was such an overwhelming feeling. I had never fed anyone before this. *I think feeding your loved ones is extremely under-rated. It should be encouraged. It hits you differently.* It can't be described.

'Brother, any updates on fistula?' I questioned the ward boy.

'Yes. Surgery will begin in an hour or so,' he informed.

AV Fistula is a surgically created vein. It is made by connecting an artery to a vein in the arm usually at the wrist. It takes around 2-3 months for the fistula to be ready for dialysis. Until then a catheter is used.

<u>Day 5</u>

'The surgeon will check in a bit if the fistula is developing alright and if it is, we will discharge your patient soon, we will let you know in a while,' this was Dr. Hans's words, Pradeep uncle notified us.

The room was pretty loaded today. We didn't find any space. Uncle kept roaming in the aisle after relaying the information. Being a tad overweight, mamiji found it difficult to stand for too long. She decided to take a chance. She noted few kids occupying chairs. Without wasting any time, she walked up to the lady sitting between the 2 kids.

'Ye aapke bacche hain?' she investigated.

'Yes,' she replied.

'Apne saath bithaie inko,' she ordered.

The lady made sour faces while hoisting up a kid to adjust him on her lap.

Mamiji gestured me to come in.

I accepted the seat gleefully. A look of triumph was vividly noticeable on her face.

'Usko bhi uthaie,' she demanded.

I could sniff the trouble.

'Jyada drama naa kar,' the lady responded with vengeance this time.

I knew where it was going.

'Aap yahan baithie mamiji,' I stood up immediately.

Mamiji accepted my offer, maffling something underneath her breath.

'Mr. Raju's attendant, come to room no. 124'. The speaker came to life once again.

Pradeep uncle went upstairs signaling me to stay ready in case they discharged us.

I have never been a fan of endings; endings of heartfelt experiences. Be it the ending of a good movie, a good conversation, a good relation, a good journey or anything that touches my heart. Endings take away a chunk of my heart. Endings keep needling me for a while. I get a tad emotional. It's strange, I know, but that's how it is.

While standing in the corner, leaning back on a wall, I oscillated in the memory of last few days. I recalled the important lessons I have learnt here. I felt an unusual sort of connection with this place. I was overcome with nostalgia for my days in this waiting room.

My phone rang.

'Clear all the bills. I will be downstairs in 15 minutes with your mama,' Uncle notified me.

After breaking this good news to mamiji, I squirreled towards the billing counter.

When I returned to the room, I saw mamaji on a wheelchair, his eyes half open, uncle standing beside him, mamiji rooted to the chair.

While leaving the waiting room, I noticed a pair of black shoes kept on the L corner seat.

CHAPTER X

The Last Meeting

कुछ शामें यूँ भी गुज़ारी हैं हमने
थोड़े बे-सुध, थोड़े ख़ुश, थोड़े नम

He was at the Durga restaurant.

He had already secured a curtained, corner cabin which could not be monitored from outside. She zoomed in. After a delay of 20 minutes. Settled herself on his left. No greetings. No hug. No kiss. No eye contact. Usually, whenever they used to meet, she greeted him either with a hug or a kiss. Then again, this was not the usual meeting in any sense.

A cascade of emotions struck him: He felt relieved on her arrival; He felt restless anticipating her departure. He felt anxious imagining the upcoming conversation. He felt bizarre about the forthcoming changes. He felt terror of losing her.

He waited, drinking in the sight of her.

She wiped the condensation from her glass.

He waited for her to initiate the conversation as she had promised when they had chatted last time.

'Ab jo bolna hai milke hi bolungi,' she had said.

She didn't say anything. He noticed a drop of tear strolling down the bridge of her nose.

'Milungi tab dekhna meri haalat,' she had warned him.

Call it a weakness, stupidity or flimsy, he absolutely hated to see her cry. No matter what she had done with him. Tears in her eyes was something he could not afford to see. He pulled out his handkerchief from his pocket and swiped off those precious little pearls.

'Please, don't cry,' his eyes welled up too. 'Let's order something first and then we'll talk,' he suggested with the hope that it will change her mood.

For her, good food was synonymous to joy. He was alive to this fact. He reached for a laminated menu sandwiched between a metal napkin holder and bottles of ketchup.

Sliding the menu toward her, 'you pick', he said. 'I trust you.'

In the interim, he fondly remembered the time when he had a cup of tea with her (for the very first time in his life) only to see her eyes glitter. And once, they had a dispute regarding the non-vegetarian food she would be required to give up after their marriage. She had expressed her dissent against it saying 'why should she make all the sacrifices all the time?' She hadn't calm down until he acceded to her offer of eating non-veg food once. Yes, he did agree. He loved her way too much and if eating non-veg food could prove his love for her, he was not going to balk.

As soon as the waiter vanished, he twirled towards her, interlocking his hands into hers, he asked earnestly, 'bol na! tu kya kehne wali thi?'

Her effort to evade eye contact was clearly visible to him.

'Is there anything left to say? You have already declared me a traitor!' she said in a subdued voice.

'Let me tell you one thing dear, I have never assumed anything. Even if all the evidence were bawling against you, I preferred cross-examining them. And on calls, you tended to dodge my questions. That is why I was aching to have this meeting. I hope you can sense how dismantled I am right now,' he responded in a melancholic tone.

'Alright. Tell me precisely, what do you want to know?' She countered, breaking the lock of his hand, spooning the mobile phone out of her pocket and dumping it on the table.

'Why didn't you tell me that your ex is back in your life? Why didn't you tell me that you went to meet him 2 days ago?'

Lies have always been a prime threat to the life of any relationship.

'Because, I thought you are already stressed due to your unsettled career and I didn't want to add to your trouble. I thought I would handle him on my own. I didn't want to bother you.'

He evaluated her reply, wondering whether to believe her. 'Oh! And what answer do you have for this? Not that the sex matters but why did you keep your past sexual relationship with your ex a secret?'

'You already gave the answer. Because it never really mattered to you.'

'Yes. Virginity never really mattered to me. Having said that, the lie matters. I hate lies, you know that. And the recent discovery of your series of lies makes me wonder if your love was a complete lie? if you have loved me even for a moment? It makes me wonder how many times you might have lied to me in these 12 months?'

'Hmm. I agree. I shouldn't have lied. I made a serious blunder.' No defensiveness in her tone, he noted, just the truth. He liked that.

The waiter rushed in carrying a basket of naan, together with, a cauldron of dum aaloo.

She arranged them into a plate, picked up a morsel and offered it to him.

For the moment, he elected to put his exasperation aside. 'You have finally learnt how to feed someone properly,' he said, gobbling it up.

'I think so', she half-smiled.

'And what a pity!! It would be the last time that I am getting fed by you,' he mourned before putting a morsel in her mouth.

He had a baffling hunger of feeding her. He loved those moments when he used to take a morsel in his hand and wait while she blabbered her stories or fiddled with her cell phone.

'So what next? Is it really the last time? Do we have anything left between us?' he blurted out the dreaded question hesitantly.

'I can't stay in this relationship anymore. I don't think you trust me anymore. And I don't think you will ever be able to.' He felt a pit form in his stomach.

'So you have decided to leave! Haan?'

'Haan.'

'What about those promises of staying together till the last breath?' He fought back his tears.

Her phone buzzed.

She declined it.

'You will always be with me na. Aap toh mere andar hi ho bas ab saath rehna possible nahi hai.'

Her phone buzzed again.

She declined it again.

'Why don't you pick up the call? Whose call is it?'

'From my coaching institute,' she swallowed a lump.

'Naam toh hoga kuch?'

Sensing the precariousness of the situation, she corrected her lie. It was from her Ex-boyfriend.

He felt a knot form in his chest. 'Can you do me a favor?' he solicited.

'What?'

'Look into my eyes and promise me, you will never hurt someone else after this. Promise me that you will never break someone's heart again. Can you?'

Reluctantly, she looked into his eyes and said, 'I will try but I can't guarantee'.

'Okay. Just one more request. Can you kiss me one last time?'

No sooner than he made the request, the lights went out.

She grabbed him by his collar and kissed him hard and long on his lips, similar to what they had always discussed.

As soon as she finished, the lights came in. As if the whole universe had conspired this scene.

It was the time to say goodbye now. Perhaps for the last time.

Leaping forward, he enveloped her, laying down his head on her chest, 'don't go, please. I don't want to live without you'.

She held herself back for a couple of seconds, stood up and left without saying a word.

He remained lying on the chair in the puddle of tears.

Hope you had a great time:)

Don't forget to pass your invaluable feedback at ashucric95@gmail.com

You can also follow and DM Aashu on instagram @ Kandoi95

His other works:

1. SOFT CORNER - essence of being human (english)

2. KYA HUWA TERA VADA (hindi)

www.ingramcontent.com/pod-product-compliance
Lightning Source LLC
Chambersburg PA
CBHW020457160726
47991CB00007B/2702